INK OF THE IRREVERSIBLE

A philosophical adventure novel about life being a book whose pages cannot be turned back.

Nitin Narendra Jawale (KRG)

NJPOSTS.CO

NJPOSTS.co

The danger isn't what might happen. It's what has already started.

-ARIN VALE

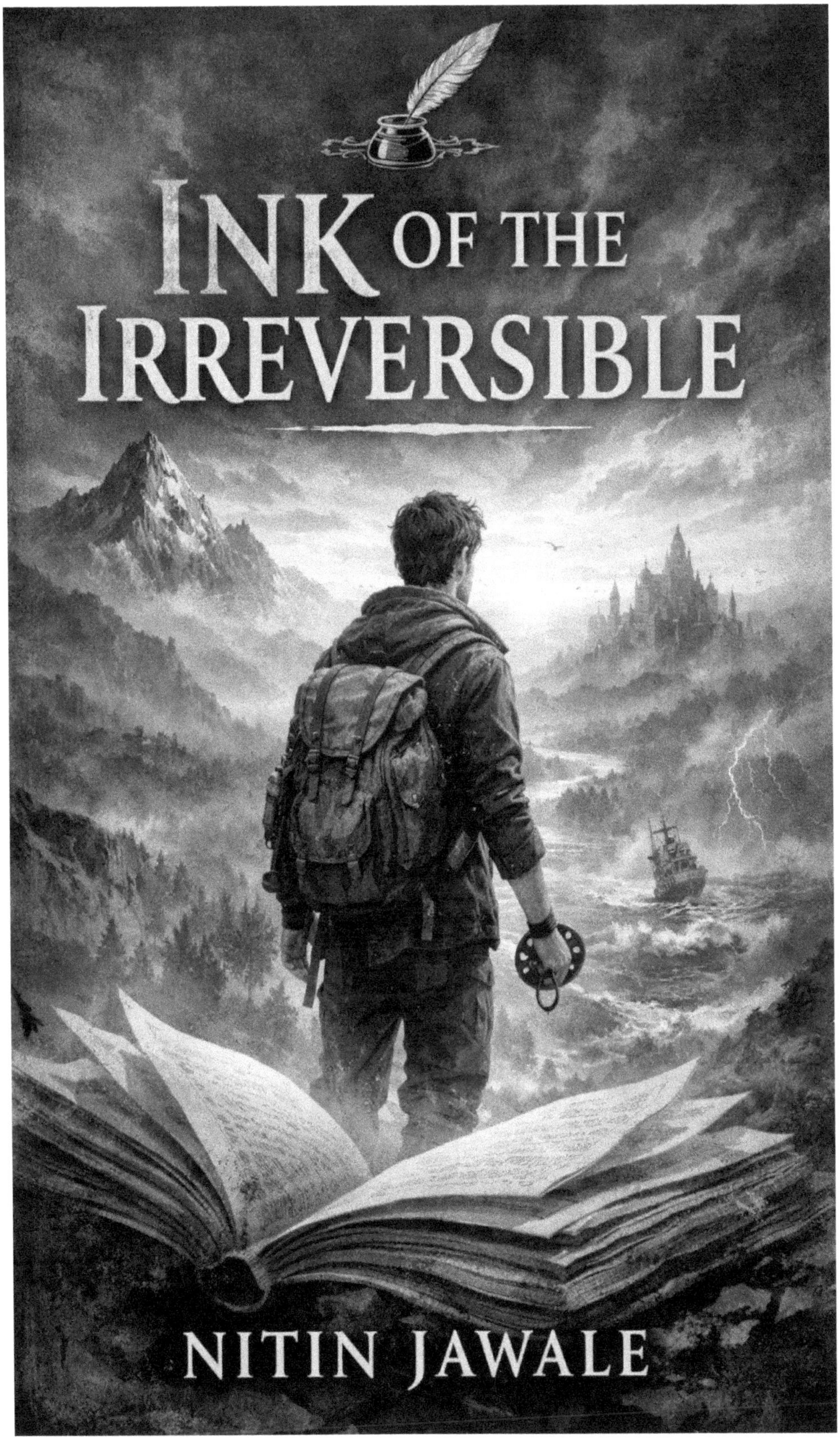
INK OF THE
IRREVERSIBLE
NITIN JAWALE

Concept Creator: Nitin Narendra Jawale (KRG)

Title: Ink of the Irreversible

Date Created: 12 March 2026

This is a work of fiction. Names, characters, businesses, places, events, and incidents are either the product of the author's imagination or used fictitiously. Any resemblance to actual persons, living or dead, or actual events is purely coincidental.

First Edition: 2026 (Revision 1)

ISBN: 978-93-5782-713-3

Printed and distributed worldwide.

Dedication

For those who understand that life is not measured by the number of pages written, but by the awareness with which they are written.

Preface

Every human life is a book already in progress.

It begins long before we understand its meaning, and it continues to write itself with every decision we make.

Unlike the books we read, this one contains no eraser.

No revision.

No returning to the previous page.

Every word spoken becomes ink.

Every choice becomes history.

Every moment lived becomes permanent.

Many people live as if they will one day rewrite their past.

But life moves only forward.

The pages turn whether we are ready or not.

This story follows a man who began his journey believing that life offered endless chances to correct mistakes.

What he discovered instead was something far more powerful:

The awareness that every moment is sacred precisely because it cannot be lived again.

Table of Contents

12. The Reader of His Own Life

CHAPTER 1 - THE DECISION TO LEAVE

(Part 1 — The Weight of Stillness)

The silence in Ellmere was not a void. It was a physical weight, a thick, invisible silt that had settled over the valley for centuries, muffling the sharp edges of existence.

Arin Vale woke before the sun, as he had for ten thousand mornings, not because of an alarm or a purpose, but because his body was a clock whose gears had been worn smooth by repetition. He lay staring at the ceiling of his bedroom. He knew every hairline fracture in the plaster. There was one above his head that looked like a reaching hand, and another near the window that resembled a lightning bolt frozen in mid-strike. They hadn't changed in twenty-eight years. In Ellmere, even the cracks in the walls seemed to have lost the ambition to grow.

He sat up, the floorboards groaning under his weight. It was a tired sound—the sigh of wood that had forgotten the forest.

He moved to the window.

The town below was draped in a pre-dawn Gray, the colour of a faded photograph left too long in the sun. Ellmere sat in the palm of the valley, ringed by hills that felt less like geography and more like the rim of a bowl. Nothing ever spilled out; nothing ever climbed in.

He watched the baker, Mr. Halloway, step onto the cobblestones to hang the iron pretzel sign above his door. Halloway's movements were rhythmic, robotic. He didn't look at the sky. He didn't check the wind. He simply performed the choreography of a life he had inherited from a father who had performed it before him.

"Is he happy?" Arin whispered, his voice sounding abrasive in the absolute quiet of the room.

The question drifted away, unanswered. Happiness required a contrast—a peak to measure against a valley. In Ellmere, there were no peaks. There was only the Level. The Great Middle. A life lived in the amber of "just enough."

The Anatomy of a Hill

Arin sat at his small wooden desk. The wood was scarred with nicks from his childhood; marks he had made when he still possessed the energy to be restless.

He looked at the hill.

It was a singular, unremarkable mound of earth on the eastern edge of the town. It was covered in a pale, sickly grass that never seemed to turn truly green in the spring or truly brown in the winter. It just... endured.

He had counted his glances at that hill. Three thousand. It was a lie he told himself to feel like he was keeping track of his own erosion. In reality, the number was likely closer to a million. Every time he looked at it, he felt a phantom pressure in his lungs, as if the hill were sitting on his chest. It represented the horizon of his entire world. To the people of Ellmere, the hill was the end of the earth. Beyond it lay the "Out," a place spoken of in the same way one speaks of a ghost—something that might have existed once but was no longer relevant to the living.

Time did not pass here, Arin thought, his fingers tracing the edge of his desk. *It hovered.*

He imagined time as a thick mist clinging to the cobblestones. In other places—the places in the old, forbidden books—time was a river. It tore things down; it carried things away; it transformed. But here, time was a stagnant pond. The clocktower in the square chimed six times. The sound was hollow, the ghost of a bell. The tower had been broken and mended so many times that it was no longer a clock; it was a monument to the refusal to let things break.

The Journal: An Act of Treason

Then, his eyes fell on the object that didn't belong.

The journal.

It sat in the centre of his desk like a fallen meteorite. It was a deep, bruised brown, the leather smelling of oil and distance. He had bought it three days ago from a traveller—a man with dusty boots and eyes that moved too fast for Ellmere. The man had stayed only an hour, long enough to trade the book for a meal, and then he was gone, vanishing toward the hills before the Sun-Watchers could ask him his business.

To own something new in Ellmere was an act of quiet rebellion. Everything else Arin owned had a lineage. His bed had belonged to his grandfather. His spoons were stamped with the crest of a great-uncle. His very name was a recycled sound.

But this journal was blank.

He touched the cover. The leather felt warm, almost as if it had a pulse. It was the only thing in the room that didn't feel like a memory.

He opened it.

The pages were a creamy white, startlingly bright against the dim light of the room. They weren't just paper; they were an invitation. An empty room. A door left ajar.

Arin felt a sudden, sharp pang of vertigo. For twenty-eight years, he had lived a life of "Waiting." He had waited for his life to start, waited for a girl to look at him differently, waited for a

Great Event to shake the valley.

But as he stared at the blankness, he realized the most terrifying truth of his existence:

The silence of Ellmere wasn't waiting for him to join it. It was waiting for him to disappear into it.

If he sat here for another twenty years, he would eventually become Mr. Halloway. He would hang a sign. He would walk the same six paces to the well. He would grow into the shape of his father until the two of them were indistinguishable, and then he would die, and his son would step into the mold he left behind.

His hand began to tremble. It wasn't the shaking of a coward. It was the vibration of a machine being turned on for the first time in a century.

He picked up the pen. The nib was sharp. The ink well was full of dark, liquid potential.

If I write one word, he realized, *the silence is broken. If I write one word, I am no longer a part of the echo.*

He leaned forward, his heart hammering against his ribs like a trapped bird. The air in the room felt suddenly thin, as if the town itself were trying to hold its breath, sensing a fracture in the foundation.

He pressed the pen to the paper.

The ink bled into the fibers—black, permanent, and defiant.

Today I begin.

(Part 2 — The Ghost Walk)

The ink was still wet on the page, a glistening black wound in the center of the white, when Arin stood. He didn't close the journal yet. He let the words—Today I begin—stare back at him, accusing him of a promise he wasn't entirely sure he could keep.

The air in the room felt different now. The stillness was no longer passive; it felt watchful. Every object he owned seemed to pulse with a sudden, heavy significance. His chair, the wash-basin, the small wooden carving of a bird his father had given him—they weren't just things. They were anchors. They were part of a vast, invisible web designed to keep him exactly where he was.

He moved to the corner of the room and pulled a canvas rucksack from beneath his bed. It was stiff with age and smelled of cedar and neglected dreams.

Packing was an exercise in soul-searching. In a life of twenty-eight years, what was worth the weight of a climb?

He folded a heavy wool tunic—the one his mother had knitted, her fingers moving in the same repetitive rhythm that governed the whole town. He hesitated, then tucked in a small, sharp paring knife. It was a tool of utility, but in the context of Ellmere, it felt like a weapon. He added a loaf of dense, dark bread he'd taken from the larder, wrapping it in a linen cloth.

Finally, he reached for the journal.

As his fingers brushed the leather, a wave of cold flashed through him. To take the journal was to take the future. To leave it was to die here. He slid it into the center of the pack, cushioned by his clothes, like a beating heart protected by ribs.

The Threshold

Arin stood at his front door. His hand rested on the iron latch. It was cool and pitted with age, the metal worn smooth by generations of Vales who had entered and exited this house, always returning, always staying within the lines.

He closed his eyes and listened.

From the street below, he heard the rhythmic *thwack-thwack* of a broom. That would be Mrs. Gable. She swept her doorstep every morning at 6:15 AM. She had done so for forty years. She didn't sweep because there was dirt; she swept because it was 6:15.

If he opened this door, he would step into that rhythm. He would see her. She would nod—a stiff, practiced movement—and he would be expected to nod back. That nod was a contract. It said: *I am here, you are there, and nothing has changed.*

"I'm not coming back," he whispered.

The house didn't answer. It couldn't. It was made of Ellmere stone and Ellmere wood, and it didn't understand the concept of 'away.'

He pressed down the latch. The click sounded like a bone breaking.

The Walk Through the Echoes

The street was a canyon of muted colors. The fog had begun to lift, but it lingered in the doorways like uninvited guests. Arin walked with his head down, his pack feeling heavier with every step. It wasn't the physical weight; it was the gravity of the town pulling at his heels.

He passed the well in the center of the square. A group of men stood there, their breath blooming in the chill air. They weren't talking about the world or the future. They were discussing the repair of a fence, their voices low and melodic, circling the same three points they had discussed the week before.

As Arin passed, one of them—Old Man Thorne—looked up. His eyes were clouded, the color of dishwater. For a second, his gaze locked onto Arin's rucksack.

The rhythm of the sweeping stopped. The men at the well fell silent.

It was a soft silence, but it was terrifying. It was the sound of a hive noticing a bee flying in the wrong direction.

"Early start, Arin?" Thorne called out. The words were friendly, but the tone was heavy with a subtle, crushing pressure. It wasn't a question; it was a reminder. *You belong in the pattern. Why are you out of step?*

"Just a walk, Mr. Thorne," Arin said, his throat tight.

He didn't stop. He couldn't. If he stopped, the conversation would wrap around him like ivy. They would ask about his father. They would mention the weather. They would slowly, politely, pull him back into the Great Middle until the sun was high and the urge to leave had withered into a dull ache of "maybe tomorrow."

He quickened his pace. The cobblestones under his boots felt slick, as if the road itself were trying to trip him.

The Narrow Way

The road out of Ellmere was a psychological barrier as much as a physical one. It narrowed as it left the square, squeezed by the encroaching gray-green hills.

Here, the town began to fray. The houses were older, their windows like squinting eyes. The grass grew tall and pale, reaching across the path as if to stitch the earth back together.

Arin reached the Great Milestone—a hunk of granite that marked the official edge of the town's jurisdiction. Beyond this point, the "Quiet" of Ellmere changed. It was no longer the quiet of a sleeping house; it was the silence of a wilderness that didn't know his name.

He stopped. His heart was a drum in his ears.

Behind him lay the safety of the known. He could turn around right now, go home, put the bread back in the larder, and no one would ever mention his rucksack. He could live another fifty years in the comfort of the echo. He would never be hungry. He would never be lost. He would also never be alive.

He looked toward the mountains. They were jagged teeth against a bruised sky. They looked indifferent. Cold.

What if the world ends there? the doubt hissed in the back of his mind. *What if Ellmere is the only bubble of air in a universe of suffocating nothingness?*

He reached back and felt the hard shape of the journal through the canvas of his pack.

Empty vs. Blank, he reminded himself.

The world wasn't empty. It was just waiting for him to write it.

Arin Vale took a breath—a real, deep breath that burned his lungs with the sharp scent of pine and damp earth—and stepped past the milestone.

He didn't look back. He knew that if he saw the smoke rising from Mr. Halloway's chimney, or the familiar slant of his own roof, the gravity would become too much to fight. He kept his eyes on the mountains, watching as the soft, rolling hills began to sharpen into the world's end.

(Part 3 — The Hills of Doubt)

The transition was not a single moment, but a slow, agonizing erosion.
For the first mile, Ellmere clung to his heels. He could still hear the distant, rhythmic tolling of the clocktower—a faint, metallic heartbeat pulsing through the valley floor. He could still smell the ghost of coal smoke and yeast. It was as if the town were a living entity with invisible cilia, reaching out to snag his clothes, to whisper familiar names into the cup of his ear.

Then, the road simply... ceased.

It didn't end in a grand gate or a sudden cliff. It just dissolved. The cobblestones gave way to packed earth, then to gravel, and finally to a narrow, hesitant ribbon of dirt that seemed embarrassed to exist. The grass here was different—no longer the manicured, defeated green of the town squares, but a wild, pale straw that hissed against his shins.

Arin stopped. The silence here was different. In Ellmere, silence was a lack of noise. Here, it was a presence. It was a vast, cold weight that lived in the gaps between the trees and the hollows of the rocks. It didn't care about his history. It didn't know his name.

For the first time in twenty-eight years, Arin Vale was irrelevant.

The Scale of the Mountain

He looked up. The mountains, which had been distant, painted backdrops for his entire life, had suddenly become three-dimensional. They were no longer shapes; they were gods.

Their peaks were jagged, obsidian teeth that tore at the belly of the clouds. They were ancient, indifferent, and massive. They made the Great Hill of Ellmere look like a child's toy. Looking at them, Arin felt a sudden, sharp spike of terror—a physical sensation like cold water being poured down his spine.

What if there is nothing?

The thought wasn't a whisper; it was a roar. The people of Ellmere always implied that the world ended at the peaks. They spoke of the "Out" as a void, a place where the air ran thin and the light died.

He looked back.

From this vantage point, Ellmere was a tiny, gray smudge in the palm of a green hand. It looked fragile. It looked safe. He could see the thin line of the road he had just walked. It looked like an umbilical cord.

One turn. One decision. He could be back in his bed by nightfall. He could tell everyone he went for a long hike. They would nod. They would accept the lie because the lie maintained the Pattern.

He reached into his bag, his fingers trembling as they found the journal. He didn't pull it out; he just gripped it. The hardness of the spine was a physical anchor in a world that was suddenly too large.

Beginning is not about knowing where you are going, he thought, the words forming in his mind like a mantra. *It is about choosing to leave where you were.*

The First Fracture

He began to walk again, but the earth was fighting him now. The incline sharpened. The air grew thinner, tasting of stone and old snow. Every step was a negotiation with gravity.

His boots, made for the flat, predictable streets of the town, slipped on the loose scree. He went down on one knee, the sharp rocks biting into his skin. He stayed there for a moment, panting, the blood hot and metallic in his mouth.

A shadow fell over him.

He looked up, expecting to see a cloud, but instead, he saw a hawk. It was a speck of burnt umber against the gray sky, circling in effortless, perfect arcs. It didn't have a map. It didn't have a history. It just existed in the tension between the wind and the earth.

Arin watched it, and a strange, hysterical laugh bubbled up in his chest.

"You don't have a clocktower, do you?" he whispered.

The hawk screamed—a thin, piercing sound that shattered the heavy silence of the hills. It was the first "new" sound Arin had heard in years. It wasn't a chime, a broom, or a greeting. It was a declaration of life.

He stood up, wiping the dirt from his palms. The pain in his knee was sharp, but it was *his* pain. It wasn't a memory of a fall he'd had as a child; it was a consequence of a choice he had made ten minutes ago.

He felt a sudden, fierce rush of adrenaline. He wasn't just walking; he was breaking. He was a crack in a frozen lake, spreading outward, irreversible and chaotic.

The Disappearance of the Path

As the sun began to dip toward the horizon, painting the peaks in shades of bruised purple and dying gold, the path vanished entirely. He was standing on a ridge, the wind whipping his hair across his eyes.

Ahead of him lay a forest of pine so dark it looked like a spill of ink across the mountainside. Behind him, the valley was swallowed by shadows. Ellmere was gone. Not hidden by a bend in the road, but erased by the sheer scale of the landscape.

It was the most terrifying moment of his life.

He was truly alone. No ancestors to guide his steps. No neighbors to judge his pace. Just a man, a loaf of bread, and a blank book.

He sat on a flat stone, the cold of the mountain seeping through his trousers. He opened the journal to that first page. The ink had dried.

Today I begin.

He took his pen and, with a hand that was finally steady, he wrote beneath it:

The town is gone. The silence is loud. I am afraid. And for the first time, I am awake.

He closed the book. The mountains loomed over him, silent and watching. They didn't welcome him. They didn't forbid him. They simply waited to see what he would do next.

Arin Vale stood up, adjusted the straps of his pack, and walked toward the dark trees.

(Part 4 — The Forest of Echoes)

The forest did not welcome him. It tolerated him, the way a giant might tolerate a flea crawling across its knuckles.

As Arin stepped beneath the canopy of the ancient pines, the temperature dropped ten degrees. The air here was thick with the scent of rot and rebirth—damp earth, pine resin so sharp it stung his throat, and the cold, metallic smell of wet stone. The light, which had been a bruised gold on the ridges, was filtered through a million needles until it became a sickly, underwater green.

Silence in the forest was not like silence in the town. In Ellmere, silence was a blanket; here, it was a sharpened blade.

Every snap of a twig under his boot sounded like a pistol shot. Every rustle of a hidden creature in the ferns made his skin prickle. He felt a gaze on the back of his neck—not the judging gaze of a neighbor, but the hungry, indifferent gaze of the wild.

The First Night: The Death of the Pattern

As the sun fully retreated, the shadows didn't just grow; they solidified. They poured out from between the trunks like spilled ink, swallowing the ground until Arin could no longer see his own feet.

He had never been in true darkness. In Ellmere, there was always a candle in a window, a lantern on a post, or the soft, reassuring glow of a hearth. Here, the darkness was absolute. It was a physical barrier.

He fumbled with his pack, his fingers numb with a creeping chill that seemed to come from the earth itself. He found a small clearing protected by a shelf of rock—a "lean-to" of nature's design.

He didn't build a fire. He didn't know how. The realization hit him with the force of a blow to the stomach. In twenty-eight years, he had never needed to provide for his own survival. Heat was something that came from a stove. Food was something that appeared on a plate.

He was a man-child, dressed in the clothes of a rebel but possessing the skills of a ghost.

He sat on the cold ground, his back against the stone, and pulled his wool tunic tight around his chest. He took out the loaf of bread. In the dark, it tasted like dust. It was the taste of Ellmere—stale, predictable, and rapidly disappearing.

The Psychological Haunting

The wind began to rise, moaning through the high branches. To Arin's ears, the sound began to morph. It sounded like Mrs. Gable's broom—thwack-thwack-thwack. Then it sounded like the rhythmic chime of the broken clocktower.

Go back, the wind seemed to whisper. You are nothing out here. You are a breath in a storm. Go back to the house with the cracked ceiling. Go back to the life that was lived for you.

He closed his eyes, but the darkness behind his eyelids was no better. He saw the faces of the men at the well. He saw the baker. He saw the hill. He realized then that leaving a place is easy; it's leaving the idea of the place that tears the skin.

He was grieving. Not for a person, but for the certainty of his own insignificance. In Ellmere, he knew exactly how he would die. Out here, he didn't even know how he would wake up.

The Journal as a Shield

He reached into his bag and pulled out the journal. He couldn't see the pages, but he ran his hand over the leather. He felt the indentation of the words he had written earlier.

Today I begin.

The words felt like a lie in the face of the towering pines and the invisible predators. But as he gripped the book, a new thought surfaced—a small, flickering candle in the drafty hall of his mind.

If I go back, he realized, I am not going back to safety. I am going back to a slow, polite execution.

He remembered the way the children in Ellmere grew into "precise versions of their parents." He saw himself thirty years from now, standing at the well, watching another young man walk away with a rucksack. He saw the gray dishwater in his own eyes.

He would rather freeze in this forest as a "Beginner" than rot in that valley as an "Echo."

The Breaking of the Dawn

He didn't sleep. He hovered in a state of hyper-vigilance, his ears straining at every hoot of an owl and every groan of a shifting branch. He felt the "environmental immersion" the prompt demanded—the way the cold seeped into his bones, the way the dampness of the forest floor felt like it was trying to claim him for the soil.

But then, the gray began to return.

It wasn't a sudden light. It was a slow thinning of the shadows. The underwater green returned to the needles. The predatory silence shifted into the morning chorus of birds—a chaotic, unpracticed symphony that didn't follow a clock.

Arin stood up. His joints screamed. His muscles were stiff as old leather. He looked at his hands; they were stained with dirt and pine sap.

He wasn't the man who had left the house twenty-four hours ago. That man was clean, certain, and asleep. This man was exhausted, dirty, and terrified.

But he was standing.

He took his pen out. In the weak, gray light of the second morning, he opened the journal. The ink from yesterday looked like a scar. Beneath his last entry, he wrote:

I survived the first night. The forest tried to talk me into returning. I didn't listen. The mountains are closer now. They look like they are waiting for me to prove I am real.

He didn't eat the rest of the bread. He saved it. He was learning the economy of the "Out."

He stepped out from under the rock shelf and looked toward the peaks. They were no longer just walls; they were the next chapter.

(Part 5 — The Silver Threshold)

By noon of the second day, the forest began to thin, not into a clearing, but into a jagged, fractured landscape of limestone and shale. The air had lost its loamy weight, replaced by a sharp, ozone-scented wind that screamed of high altitudes and melting snow. Then, he heard it.

It wasn't a sound he recognized from Ellmere. The sounds of his home were rhythmic—the clack of a loom, the thud of a closing door. This was a continuous, predatory roar, a low-frequency vibration that he felt in the soles of his boots before he heard it with his ears.

He rounded a massive, moss-slicked boulder and stopped.

The Veiled River was a ribbon of churning, glacial milk. It didn't flow; it cascaded, white water exploding against black rocks with a violence that made Arin's heart stutter. It wasn't wide—perhaps twenty paces—but it was a chasm of liquid thunder. There was no bridge. There was no shallow crossing.

In Ellmere, a road led to a destination. If a bridge was out, you waited for the town council to repair it. You went home and had tea. You waited for the world to be made safe for you.

Here, the world was indifferent to his progress.

The Decision at the Bank

Arin stood at the water's edge. The spray was a cold mist that instantly coated his tunic, turning the wool heavy and dark. He looked upriver and down. The banks were sheer, rising into vertical cliffs of slick slate.

This was the "End of the World" his neighbors had whispered about. Not a physical edge to the planet, but a point where the effort of existing outweighed the desire to continue.

I can't cross this, he thought. The doubt was a physical weight, pulling him toward the ground. I am a man who writes in a book. I am not a man who swims through ice.

He looked at his hands. They were shaking. He felt the phantom touch of the Ellmere "Stillness" again, a soft hand on his shoulder, beckoning him back to the valley where the water stayed in the wells and the days stayed in their tracks.

The Utility of the Blade

He sat on a log, his breath coming in ragged gasps. He reached into his pack, searching for the bread, but his hand brushed the small paring knife.

He pulled it out.

It was a pathetic tool for a mountain. The blade was barely four inches long, designed for peeling apples and slicing cheese in a sunlit kitchen. But as he looked at the steel, he saw his own reflection—distorted, pale, and desperate.

He looked at the trees lining the bank. They were stunted, hardy things, their roots gripping the rocks like talons.

"Expand," he whispered, the master prompt's directive echoing in the back of his mind like a ghost-writer's command. "Deepen."

He didn't just need to cross the river. He needed to cut his way out of his old skin.

He stood up and approached a stand of young, flexible saplings. For the first time in his life, he used a tool not to maintain a home, but to build a path. The knife was small, and the wood was stubborn. Every cut was a struggle. His palms blistered; the raw wood stung his eyes. He spent three hours—time that would have been spent nodding to neighbors in the square—hacking at the saplings until he had six long, sturdy poles.

He used the hem of his spare tunic, tearing the fabric into strips with the blade. He bound the poles together, his fingers clumsy and frozen, until he had a crude, heavy staff and a tether.

The Leap of Faith

The crossing was a blurred nightmare of sensory overload.

The water hit his waist like a physical blow, a cold so intense it felt like fire. The current was a living thing, a liquid beast trying to sweep his legs from under him. The roar of the river swallowed his screams.

Halfway across, his foot slipped on a mossy stone.

He went under.

The world turned into a chaotic swirl of gray and white. His lungs burned. The weight of his pack—the weight of his journal—was pulling him down into the dark.

In that moment, suspended between the life he had left and the death he had invited, Arin Vale felt a flash of absolute, crystalline clarity. He didn't want the safety of the valley. He didn't want the comfort of the echo.

He wanted the next page.

He jammed his staff into a crevice in the riverbed. The wood groaned, nearly snapping, but it held. He hauled himself upward, his muscles screaming, his vision spotting with black. He fought the river for every inch, his fingers clawing at the freezing silt of the opposite bank until he collapsed onto the dry stones.

He lay there for a long time, vomiting river water, his body racked with tremors. He was soaked, freezing, and miles from any hearth.

But he was on the other side.

The Irreversible Mark

When he could finally move, he crawled to a patch of pale sunlight hitting a flat rock. He fumbled with his pack. His heart nearly stopped until his fingers found the journal. It was wrapped in the linen of the bread, damp but not ruined.

He opened it. The ink of "Today I begin" had bled slightly at the edges, the letters looking like they were weeping.

He took his pen. His hand was no longer shaking from fear, but from the raw, electric hum of survival. He wrote, the nib digging deep into the wet paper:

The river tried to take me. I took the river instead. I have lost my bread. I have lost my warmth. But I have found my hands. They are scarred, and they are mine.

He looked up. The mountains were no longer distant gods. He was on their doorstep. And for the first time, Arin Vale realized that a story doesn't just begin with a word.

It begins with a scar.

(Part 6 — The Ossuary of Giants)

The sun was a pale, mocking coin hanging over the serrated edge of the peaks. Arin moved through the shadows of the foothills, his wet clothes clinging to him like a second, colder skin. Every gust of wind felt like a rhythmic slapping, a reminder that the mountain did not want him warm.

As he climbed, the geology changed. The limestone gave way to a dark, porous rock that looked like it had been charred by an ancient fire. And then, he saw them.

They rose from the scree like the ribs of a buried leviathan—pillars of worked stone, half-toppled and smoothed by centuries of wind. They weren't natural. They were too precise, their edges still hinting at a geometry that Ellmere had forgotten.

Arin stopped, his breath hitching in his chest. In the stories told by the elders, there was nothing beyond the hills but "The Waste." But these stones spoke of a "Before." They spoke of hands that had carved, minds that had planned, and a civilization that had dared to build where the air was thin.

The Sanctuary of Echoes

He found a gap between two leaning slabs—a natural crawlspace that offered a reprieve from the biting wind. As he edged inside, the roar of the mountain faded, replaced by a silence so profound it felt heavy.

He struck a flint he had scavenged from the riverbank, the sparks illuminating the interior.

The walls were covered in carvings.

They weren't the simple, decorative patterns of Ellmere's woodworkers. These were frantic, flowing lines—depictions of stars falling like rain, of people with eyes turned toward a horizon that didn't end in a valley.

Arin reached out, his frozen fingers tracing a carving of a Great Bird. It wasn't the hawk he had seen earlier; it was something larger, something that carried a rider.

They left, he realized. The thought hit him with the force of a physical revelation. *They didn't just stay in their valleys. They climbed. They saw.*

The Cost of the Discovery

The adrenaline of the discovery began to fade, replaced by the gnawing, hollow ache of hunger. His loaf of bread was at the bottom of the Veiled River, likely being picked apart by silver-scaled fish.

He sat on the dusty floor of the ruin, his back against the ancient carvings. He felt small. Not the "insignificant" smallness of Ellmere, where he was just a cog in a machine, but a "cosmic" smallness. He was a single heartbeat in a cathedral of dead giants.

He pulled the journal from his pack. The dampness had made the leather supple, and the pages were slightly warped, giving the book a weathered, ancient look that matched the ruins around him.

He didn't have a pen-rest or a desk. He used his thigh as a table.

The Interior World

I am sitting in the bones of a city, he wrote. His handwriting was changing—the neat, cramped script of the clerk was being replaced by something broader, more urgent.

Ellmere was not the beginning of the world. It was a hiding place. We didn't stay because it was the only place to live; we stayed because we were afraid to remember what it felt like to lose a city like this.

He paused, the scratching of his pen the only sound in the stone chamber.

My stomach is a void. My feet are bleeding. But I am looking at a map carved into a wall that no one in my town has seen for a thousand years. I am the only person alive who knows this place exists.

The realization brought a strange, cold comfort. He was the keeper of a secret. He was no longer an "Echo"; he was a "Witness."

The Shadow in the Dust

As the light outside died completely, turning the entrance of his stone sanctuary into a rectangle of star-flecked obsidian, Arin heard something.

It wasn't the wind.

It was a soft, rhythmic scraping. *Skritch. Skritch. Skritch.*

It was coming from the back of the chamber, where the darkness was absolute.

Arin froze. His hand went to the small paring knife at his belt. The blade felt pitifully short against the vast, unknown dark. He didn't breathe. He waited, his ears straining until they hummed.

A pair of eyes reflected his dying ember—not gold like a wolf's, but a pale, milky blue. They were low to the ground.

For the first time, Arin Vale wasn't just facing the mountain. He was facing the inhabitants of the "Out."

(Part 7 — The Altar of the Unseen)

The air in the stone chamber didn't just turn cold; it turned stagnant, as if the oxygen itself were being consumed by whatever watched him from the gloom.

Arin's heart wasn't a drum anymore; it was a frantic bird battering its wings against the cage of his ribs. He gripped the paring knife, the wood of the handle slick with the cold sweat of his palms. In Ellmere, the only things that moved in the dark were dreams or the occasional stray cat. This was different. This was a presence that occupied space with a predatory weight, an ancient gravity that made the very shadows feel solid.

Skritch. Skritch.

The sound was rhythmic—the sound of bone or claw dragging across ancient, dusty limestone. It was the sound of something unhurried, something that knew time was an infinite resource.

The Anatomy of Terror

The milky-blue eyes didn't blink. They remained fixed, low to the ground, reflecting the dying orange pulse of his single ember like twin moons trapped in a well. Arin felt a primal, genetic memory stir in the back of his brain—the terror of the ancestor who first realized that the cave belonged to the beast.

"I have nothing," Arin whispered, his voice a jagged sliver of sound that cracked the silence. "No food. No wealth. I am just a man who left."

The eyes shifted. They didn't retreat; they tilted, as if the creature were studying the cadence of his speech, weighing the soul behind the words.

Slowly, agonizingly, a shape began to detach itself from the obsidian shadows. It wasn't a wolf. It wasn't a bear. It was a creature of the heights—a mountain fox, but warped by the altitude and the isolation. Its fur was the color of a winter cloud, thick and matted with frozen burrs, and its ears were oversized, twitching with every frantic beat of Arin's heart.

But it was the fox's mouth that stopped Arin's breath.

It wasn't bared in a snarl. It was carrying something.

With a deliberate, almost mocking grace, the creature stepped into the faint circle of light. It dropped its burden at Arin's feet: a small mountain-hare, its fur still warm, its neck snapped with surgical precision.

The Silent Pact

Arin stared at the offering. He looked from the hare to the fox. The milky-blue eyes were no longer predatory; they were ancient. They looked like the eyes of a creature that had watched the stones fall, that had seen the "Giants" leave, and had been waiting for someone to return to the silence.

The fox didn't wait for a thank you. It didn't wag a tail. It simply turned and melted back into the shadows of the rear chamber, its presence lingering like a scent of musk and old snow.

Arin sank back against the wall, his legs finally giving out. The knife clattered to the floor, the sound echoing like a bell in a tomb.

He was starving. His body was a hollow shell of tremors and bile. He looked at the hare, then at his hands. In Ellmere, meat came wrapped in butcher's paper, clean and divorced from the life it once held. Here, survival was visceral. It was red. It was raw. It was the price of admission to the world beyond the hill.

The Conversion of the Soul

He used the paring knife.

The task was gruesome, a messy, fumbling initiation into the reality of the "Out." His hands became stained with a different kind of ink—the dark, iron-scented blood of the mountain. He didn't have a fire to cook it, but the desperation of his cells overrode the sensibilities of the townsperson.

He ate.

It was the most honest meal of his life. It tasted of salt and effort. It tasted of the end of his innocence. As he chewed, his eyes wandered back to the carvings on the wall—the stars falling like rain, the Great Birds with their riders. He realized then that the fox hadn't brought him food out of kindness. It had brought him a test.

To stay in the ruins, he had to become part of the ruin's ecosystem. He had to stop being a guest and start being a tenant. He had to stop being a man of Ellmere and start being a man of the Mountain.

The Journal: A New Vocabulary

He pulled the journal toward him. His fingers were stained, and when he touched the paper, he left a smudge of copper-red across the corner of the page. He didn't try to wipe it away. It was the first authentic mark of his journey.

I am eating the mountain, he wrote. The words felt heavy, tectonic.

The "Stillness" of Ellmere was a lie told to keep us from the hunger. But hunger is where the truth lives. I am no longer afraid of the dark. I am afraid of the man who would have stayed in the light and starved without ever knowing why.

He looked toward the rectangle of stars framed by the stone entrance. The "Ossuary of Giants" wasn't a tomb; it was a nursery. It was where the old world had laid its eggs, waiting for someone with enough hunger to crack the shells.

He closed his eyes, and for the first time since he had closed his front door in the valley, he slept. He didn't dream of the clocktower or the baker's sign. He dreamed of wings.

The sun did not rise over the mountains; it ignited them.

Arin woke to a world of blinding white and crystalline blue. The "Ossuary of Giants" was no longer a tomb of shadows; it was a cathedral of light. The carvings on the walls, once frantic and hidden, now seemed to vibrate with a solar energy, the lines of the falling stars etched so deep they held the morning glow like liquid gold.

His body was a map of new sensations. His joints were stiff, his muscles ached with the memory of the river, and his hands were stained with the dried copper of the hare. But as he stood, he didn't feel the "Stillness." He felt a strange, electric lightness—the feeling of a tether that had finally snapped.

(Part 8 — The Horizon of the Forgotten)

He left the stone sanctuary without looking back. The fox was gone, leaving only a single, silver-white hair on the dusty floor as proof of the night's pact.

The final ascent was a vertical dialogue between bone and stone. There was no path here, only the "Intent" the prompt demanded. Arin climbed not with the grace of a mountaineer, but with the desperation of a man who knew that if he stopped, the gravity of Ellmere would find him again. He used his cracked fingernails to find purchase in the schist. He used the small paring knife as a piton, jamming the blade into crevices to haul his weight upward.

The air was thin now, tasting of ancient ice and nothingness. His lungs burned, a sharp, clean fire that scoured the last of the valley's stagnant mist from his chest.

The Crest of the World

Then, the ground leveled out.

Arin took the final step and stood on the spine of the world.

For a moment, his brain refused to process what his eyes were seeing. In Ellmere, the horizon was a bowl. You looked up to see the edge. Here, for the first time in twenty-eight years, Arin looked *down*.

The mountains did not end in a void. They did not drop off into a black waste.

Beyond the peaks lay a sea of gold—a vast, rolling savanna that stretched so far the horizon curved into a hazy, sapphire mist. It was a world of scale he had never imagined. There were rivers that looked like silver veins, forests that appeared as patches of deep emerald velvet, and in the far distance, the shimmering, impossible ghost of a city made of white stone and glass, catching the sun like a fallen star.

It was the "Out." And it was beautiful.

The Death of the Old Map

Arin sank to his knees, not from exhaustion, but from the sheer weight of the truth.

Everything he had been told was a lie. The "Stillness" wasn't a protection; it was a blindfold. The elders hadn't kept the town safe from the world; they had kept the world safe from the town. They were afraid of the scale. They were afraid of the wind that didn't have a name.

He pulled the journal from his pack. He opened it to the very last page he had written on. The smudge of blood was dry now, a dark brown seal of his survival.

He didn't write about his fear. He didn't write about his hunger.

He wrote the only thing that mattered.

The world is not a memory, his pen flew across the paper, the ink bold and jagged. *It is a promise. I can see the end of the silence from here. It looks like light.*

The Finality of the Step

He stood on the precipice, the wind whipping his cloak—the one his mother had knitted—around his legs. He looked back one last time. He couldn't even see the valley now. The clouds had rolled in below the peaks, a white, fluffy shroud that buried Ellmere and everyone in it.

He wasn't angry at them. He felt a profound, quiet pity. They were still sweeping the porches. They were still checking the clocktower. They were still living the same day, over and over, while the sun was currently painting a masterpiece across a continent, they didn't believe in.

Arin Vale tightened the straps of his pack. He felt the weight of the journal against his spine—no longer a burden, but a compass.

He took a step. Then another.

He began the descent into the light.

The story of the man who left was over. The story of the man who arrived had just begun.

CHAPTER 2 - THE MOUNTAIN OF EFFORT

(Part 1 — The Kingdom of Indifference)

Three days.

In Ellmere, three days was the time it took for a loaf of bread to go stale or for a minor rumor to travel from the bakery to the well. Out here, under the shadow of the Ironcrest Mountains, three days was an eternity of re-learning how to breathe.

Arin Vale stood at the base of the range, his neck straining as he looked up. These were not the soft, rolling hills of his youth. The Ironcrests were a violence of geology—vast, immovable, and utterly indifferent to the fact that a man from a quiet valley was currently standing in their shadow, trembling.

The peaks didn't just rise; they pierced. They were jagged, obsidian blades that seemed to be carving the sky itself. At their summits, the morning sun struck the ice, turning the ridges into veins of molten gold that hurt to look at. But below, where Arin stood, the world was trapped in a permanent, bruised twilight. The mountain refused to reveal its full truth all at once; it kept its secrets in the deep, blue shadows of its canyons.

For the first time since he had closed his front door, Arin felt small.

It wasn't the "smallness" of being ignored by a neighbor or being a nameless face in a crowd. This was a structural revelation. It was the smallness of a single grain of sand realizing it was standing at the foot of a desert. It didn't diminish him—it stripped away the vanity of his previous life.

I am nothing to this stone, he thought, his hand instinctively gripping the strap of his pack. *And because I am nothing, I can be anything.*

The First Ascent: The Tax of the Stone

The ground beneath his boots was the first to challenge him. In Ellmere, the paths were predictable, worn smooth by centuries of the same footsteps. Here, the earth was alive and spiteful.

As he took his first step upward, the mountain moved.

Loose shale hissed beneath his weight, sliding away like a retreating wave. Sharp, flinty edges pressed through the worn leather soles of his boots—boots meant for cobblestones, not the spine of the world. Every step was a negotiation. The path didn't exist; it had to be hallucinated. It twisted in broken fragments, appearing for a few yards before diving into a cluster of jagged boulders or vanishing over a sheer drop.

The Ironcrests demanded a tax: absolute presence.

In the valley, Arin could walk for miles while his mind wandered to old memories or future anxieties. Here, a wandering thought was a death sentence. To look away from his footing was to invite a broken ankle. To lose focus was to slip into the void.

Every step is a decision, he realized, his thigh muscles beginning to hum with a low, electric heat. *And every decision has a price.*

The Challenger in the Air

Then came the wind.

It didn't blow the way valley winds did—fragrant with grass and slowing as it hit the trees. This wind arrived like a physical challenger, a cold, relentless wall of air that struck him in the chest. It carried the dry, metallic scent of ancient stone and something older—the smell of thin air and forgotten altitudes.

It whistled through the gaps in his wool tunic, clawing at his balance, trying to peel him off the face of the rock like a dead leaf.

Arin leaned into it. He didn't fight it with a scream or a push; he adjusted. He lowered his center of gravity, his fingers hooking into a narrow crevice in the granite. He was learning the mountain's language. It wasn't a dialogue; it was an interrogation. The mountain was asking: *How much do you want this?*

The Fire Within

Hours passed, but time had no meaning in the ascent. It was stretched thin across the rhythm of his lungs.

His muscles didn't just ache; they burned with a deep, consuming fire. It was a hunger of the marrow, a sensation of his own body consuming itself to provide the energy for the next lift, the next grip. His hands, once the soft hands of a man who held only pens and spoons, were now mapped with thin, angry lines of red. The rock was abrasive, a giant file that was slowly wearing him down to his essential parts.

His breath grew heavy. Then raw. Then loud.

It was the only sound in the world—the ragged, rhythmic rasp of air entering a body that was finally, truly alive. In Ellmere, he had breathed because his heart beat. Here, he breathed because his soul demanded it.

The Stripping of the Illusion

By midday, the mountain had performed its first surgery. It had stripped him of his last remaining illusion: the belief that effort alone was enough.

In the books he had read, the hero climbed until he reached the top, driven by pure will. But as Arin clung to a narrow ledge, his forehead pressed against the cold, unyielding stone, he realized that will was just the fuel. The engine was something else.

This wasn't a climb he could simply "push" through. It was a transformation he had to endure.

He paused, his chest heaving. Below him, the world had changed. The green valley of the foothills was a distant, hazy memory, a place that belonged to a different man. Above him, the summit glowed—a crown of fire and ice.

It was closer now. Close enough to believe in.

He reached for a handhold, his fingers finding a notch in the limestone.

Step. Grip. Pull. Balance.

The rhythm became his entire universe. Thought faded. Memory died. There was only the stone, the wind, and the next inch.

And then—a sound.

It didn't belong to the wind. It didn't belong to the stone. It was a fracture in the absolute silence of the heights.

"Help..."

Arin froze. The mountain seemed to hold its breath with him.

The sound had been thin, unraveling, but it was undeniably human. It was the sound of a life reaching its limit.

Arin turned, his eyes scanning the jagged outcrops of rock. There, wedged between two sharp teeth of granite, lay a shape that shouldn't be there.

A man. Broken.

The summit was right there, glowing with the promise of his new life. But the voice was down here, in the dirt.

(Part 2 — The Crucible of Mercy)

Arin moved toward the shape, his movements no longer driven by the rhythm of the ascent, but by a sudden, jagged uncertainty. Every step toward the outcrop felt like a betrayal of the altitude he had earned. The loose stones beneath his boots threatened to betray him, skittering into the abyss as if the mountain itself were trying to shake him back onto his path.

As he drew closer, the details sharpened with a brutal, high-definition clarity.

The man was older—perhaps the age Arin's father would have been if he had ever dared to leave his porch. His clothes were not the sturdy wool of the valley, but a patchwork of canvas and hide, now torn and dust-streaked until they looked like the remnants of a flag from a forgotten war.

His face was a mask of grime and agony, his lips cracked into parched canyons. But it was the leg that stopped Arin's heart. It was pinned beneath a fallen slab of granite, bent at an angle that defied the natural geometry of the human frame. The skin around the break was a terrifying shade of mottled purple, swollen and tight against the fabric of his trousers.

"Please..." the man whispered. The word was barely a vibration in the air, a fraying thread of sound. "I can't... I can't get down."

Arin crouched beside him. The heat of his own exertion met the cold, clammy radiation of the man's shock.

"What's your name?" Arin asked. His own voice sounded foreign to him—thick with the altitude, rough with the salt of his sweat.

"...Tomas."

The name was a small thing, but it changed everything. In Ellmere, names were labels; here, a name was a weight. Once a thing had a name, it could no longer be ignored.

The Siren Call of the Peak

Arin stood up slowly, his knees popping like dry twigs. He looked up.

The summit was right there.

In the deepening gold of the afternoon, the peak seemed to be burning with an internal fire. It was no longer a destination; it was a promise. It represented everything he had left Ellmere to find: Achievement. Individuality. The "End" of the Effort. He could almost feel the wind at the very top—a wind that would wash away the smell of the valley forever.

He was so close. An hour, perhaps two, of focused climbing and he would be the man who conquered the Ironcrests.

"Help me down," Tomas gasped, his hand reaching out. His fingers were like talons, gripping the hem of Arin's tunic with a desperate, terrifying strength. "I won't survive here. Not the night. The cold... it comes for the bone first."

Arin looked at the hand. Then at the summit.

Two directions. Up, toward the sun and the self. Down, toward the shadows and the burden.

The Voice of the Valley

"If you stop now," a voice whispered inside his mind—a voice that sounded like the polished, logical echo of the Ellmere elders—"you lose everything. You didn't leave your home to become a pack animal for a stranger. This is *your* story. *Your* beginning."

The logic was surgical. It was the same logic that kept the baker at his oven and the sweeper at her door. It was the logic of self-preservation. To carry Tomas down was to undo three days of agony. It was to throw away the gold of the summit for the gray of the foothills.

"You didn't come this far to turn back," the voice hissed, louder now, competing with the roar of the mountain wind. "You didn't survive the river to die on a ledge with a broken old man."

Arin's hand moved instinctively to his pack, feeling the hard, rectangular shape of the journal through the canvas.

Today I begin.

What had he begun? Was the journey about the height of the mountain, or the depth of the man? In the silence of the heights, the question felt like a physical weight, pressing against his chest harder than the thin air.

The Weight of the Journal

He didn't take the book out, but he felt the truth of it. The journal wasn't just a record of steps taken; it was a record of the soul being forged. If he reached the summit alone, leaving a man to freeze in the shadow of his achievement, what would he write on the next page?

"Today I reached the top and let a man die."

The words felt like ash in his mind. The summit would be tainted. The view would be obscured by the ghost of Tomas. He realized then that the mountain wasn't the challenge. The mountain was just a heap of stone. The real challenge was the person he was becoming while he climbed it.

"We're going down," Arin said.

The words were small, barely audible over the wind, but they carried the finality of a mountain slide.

Tomas stared at him, disbelief flickering behind the pain in his eyes. It was a look of profound, fragile hope—the look of a man who had already accepted his death and was suddenly being told he was wrong.

“Why?” Tomas asked, his voice trembling.

Arin paused. He looked at the golden light on the peak—the light he was choosing to walk away from. He thought of the "Stillness" he had escaped and the "Effort" he had embraced.

“Because,” Arin said, his voice finally steady, “I didn't leave the valley just to find a higher place to be alone.”

(Part 3 — The Gravity of Mercy)

The summit did not vanish all at once. It lingered above them, a crown of dying fire that seemed to mock Arin with every agonizing inch he retreated. To turn one's back on a peak is a physical ache, a psychic weight that pulls at the shoulders.
But Arin didn't have the luxury of looking up.

The physics of the mountain had shifted. Going up had demanded strength; going down demanded a brutal, microscopic control. Now, Arin wasn't just balancing his own life; he was an anchor for a dying man.

He had used the remains of his spare tunic and the sturdy poles he'd kept from the river crossing to fashion a makeshift drag-litter, but the terrain was too jagged for a smooth pull. Instead, he had to support Tomas, the older man's arm draped over Arin's shoulder, their bodies fused in a clumsy, limping dance of survival.

The Anatomy of the Descent

Every step was a negotiation with disaster.

The loose gravel that had been a nuisance on the way up was now a treacherous carpet of ball bearings. Arin's boots, already screaming at the seams, skidded on the slick shale. He had to jam his heels into the earth, his calves shaking with the effort of braking two hundred and fifty pounds of human weight against the relentless pull of the abyss.

The wind, sensing their vulnerability, struck with renewed malice. It didn't just push; it swirled, trying to get between them, trying to catch the loose fabric of Tomas's coat like a sail to pull them both over the ledge.

"Stay with me," Arin gritted out, the words tasting of salt and copper.

Tomas didn't answer. He was a dead weight of heat and pain, his breath a wet, ragged hitching against Arin's neck. The smell of him—old sweat, dried blood, and the sour tang of shock—filled Arin's senses, anchoring him to the brutal reality of the moment. There was no "Stillness" here. There was only the friction of skin against stone.

The Breaking Point

Halfway down the first major ridge, the mountain fought back.

A shelf of limestone, weakened by the spring melt, gave way beneath Arin's right foot. It wasn't a sudden fall; it was a slow, sickening slide.

"Hold!" Arin screamed, though there was no one to hear.

He threw his left arm out, his fingers clawing at a jagged tooth of granite. The rock bit deep, the stone slicing through his palm, but he didn't let go. He held. He became the mountain. His muscles didn't just burn; they felt as if they were being threaded with white-hot wire. For ten seconds, the world was nothing but the sound of sliding scree and the agonizing tension in his shoulder.

When the dust settled, they were dangling on the edge of a thirty-foot drop. Arin's breath came in sobbing gasps. He looked at his hand—the blood was dark and thick, mingling with the grey dust of the Ironcrests.

I could let go, the voice whispered again, fainter now, exhausted. *One slip. An accident. No one would know.*

Arin looked at Tomas. The older man's eyes had drifted open, milky and unfocused, but they settled on Arin's face for a heartbeat. There was no plea in them. Only a quiet, terrifying acceptance.

Arin hauled them back onto the ledge, his scream of effort lost in the roar of the wind.

The Sheltering Dark

Darkness didn't fall; it rose from the canyons like a predatory tide. Within minutes, the golden crown of the summit was extinguished, replaced by a cold, indigo void.

They found a narrow cut in the rock—a "scar" in the mountain's face barely wide enough for two men. It offered no warmth, only a reprieve from the wind's direct claws.

Arin collapsed against the stone, his body vibrating with a fatigue so deep it felt like a fever. He pulled Tomas close, sharing what little body heat remained in their shivering frames. The cold settled in like an uninvited truth, a silent weight that pressed against their lungs.

Tomas drifted in and out of consciousness, murmuring names of people Arin would never know. Arin stayed awake. He held the journal in his lap, though he couldn't see the pages. He ran his thumb over the cover.

He had lost the summit. He had lost the "Perfect" beginning. He was sitting in a freezing crack in the earth, covered in blood and dust, tending to a stranger.

And yet, as he listened to the mountain groan in the dark, Arin felt a strange, terrifying peace. He hadn't reached the top of the Ironcrests, but he had reached the end of the man he used to be. The effort of the descent had forged something that the easy victory of the summit never could have:

Responsibility.

The New Ink

When the sun finally touched the foothills the next morning, Arin moved with the stiff, mechanical grace of a man who had transcended pain. They reached the base of the mountains as the light turned the high peaks a mocking, beautiful pink.

He left Tomas with a group of nomadic herders at the edge of the lower woods. There were no grand speeches. No promises of eternal friendship. Only the heavy, silent look of a man who had been given a second life.

Arin stood alone once more. The Ironcrests loomed behind him, massive and indifferent as ever. He took out his journal. His hands were scarred, the skin of his palms mapped with the permanent lines of the descent.

He opened to a fresh page. He didn't look at the summit. He looked at the road ahead—a road that was now longer, harder, and entirely his own.

He wrote:

Effort reveals what matters. The summit is a destination, but the burden is a choice. I didn't reach the top today.

He paused, the pen hovering over the paper.

I reached the man instead.

(Part 4 — The Sea of Amber)

The Ironcrests did not let him go easily. For miles, the mountain range loomed behind him like a giant's spine, casting a long, cold shadow that seemed to stretch out to pull him back. Every time Arin turned to look, the peaks seemed higher, more impossible, as if mocking the fact that he had stood so close to their crown only to descend into the dust. But as the elevation dropped, the air changed.

The sharp, sterile scent of ozone and ancient ice evaporated, replaced by a thick, golden heat that smelled of sun-baked grass and a sweetness he couldn't name. It was the smell of life in its most unbridled form.

He stepped out from the last cluster of stunted pines and stopped.

Ahead of him lay the **Great Veldt**. It was a sea of amber grass, taller than a man's waist, undulating in a slow, rhythmic wave that mirrored the breathing of the earth. In Ellmere, the world ended at the hills. Here, the world seemed to have forgotten how to end. The horizon wasn't a wall; it was a suggestion, a soft sapphire curve where the gold of the earth met the pale turquoise of an endless sky.

The Cartography of a Ghost

Arin sat on a weathered stump, his body a map of his failures and his fortunes. His hands were bandaged with strips of his own tunic, the blood dried into stiff, brown crusts. He was hungry, his stomach a hollow cave, and his water skin was a shriveled leather husk.

He pulled the journal from his pack.

He didn't write immediately. Instead, he looked at the distance. From this lower vantage point, the "White City" he had seen from the summit was no longer a shimmering ghost. It was a jagged silhouette of ivory and glass, perched on the edge of a distant plateau like a crown lost in the tall grass.

Lumen, he thought. The name came to him not from a map, but from the deep, dusty corners of the stories the elders whispered when they thought the children weren't listening. The City of Light. The place where the "Giants" had gone when they grew tired of the valleys.

"It's real," he whispered, the words cracking his dry lips. "It wasn't a trick of the light."

The Arrival of the Navigator

A shadow swept over the grass, silent as a thought.

Arin reached for his paring knife—the blade now notched and dulled from the mountain—but he stopped. This wasn't the predatory weight of the forest or the indifference of the fox.

Standing ten paces away, half-submerged in the amber stalks, was a creature that looked like it had been woven from the sunset. It was a strider—a lean, flightless bird with legs like polished ebony and plumage the color of a dying fire. Its eyes were large, intelligent, and a deep, swirling violet.

It didn't flee. It tilted its head, watching him with a clinical curiosity.

Attached to its neck was a collar of braided silver, and hanging from the collar was a small, lacquered cylinder.

Arin held his breath. A collar meant a master. A master meant a civilization that didn't hide behind walls. The bird took a step forward, its movements fluid and silent, the grass parting before it as if by command. It stopped inches from Arin, the heat of its body radiating a scent of dry grain and wild musk.

The Message in the Tall Grass

With trembling fingers, Arin reached out. The bird didn't flinch. He unscrewed the cap of the cylinder. Inside was a scrap of parchment, thick and smelling of pressed flowers.

There was no writing. Only a map.

It was a single, elegant line that began at the base of the Ironcrests and wound through the Great Veldt, ending at the silhouette of the White City. At the very end of the line, a single word was embossed in silver ink:

Elias.

Arin looked from the map to the bird. The violet eyes seemed to be waiting. The bird turned, its long neck arching toward the distant plateau, and let out a low, melodic thrum that vibrated in Arin's very marrow.

The Decision to Follow

The "Effort" had changed again. On the mountain, the effort was about the *self*. In the forest, it was about *survival*. Now, it was about *destination*.

Arin stood up, his joints protesting with a chorus of pops and aches. He looked back at the Ironcrests, then ahead at the sea of gold. The White City was days away—perhaps weeks. He had no food, his boots were ruined, and he was following a bird with violet eyes toward a man he didn't know.

But as he took his first step into the amber grass, following the flicker of the bird's fire-colored feathers, Arin felt a surge of adrenaline that was cleaner than any he had felt before.

He wasn't running away anymore. He was being summoned.

He opened his journal as he walked, his pen scratching against the paper with a new, rhythmic purpose.

I have found a guide, he wrote. *Or perhaps, the world has finally found me. The mountains are behind. The city is ahead. And between them, there is only the grass and the wind.*

He looked up, watching the strider cut a path through the Veldt.

"Lead on, Elias," he murmured.

The journey to Lumen had truly begun.

(Part 5 — The Gilded Labyrinth)

The sun climbed to its zenith, turning the sky into a bowl of white-hot porcelain. Arin walked behind the strider—the bird he had begun to think of as a flicker of living flame—feeling the heat rise from the earth in shimmering, translucent waves.

The Velt was not a flat plain. It was a rhythmic series of swells and troughs, like a frozen ocean made of gold. When Arin descended into a trough, the grass rose three feet above his head, plunging him into a humid, claustrophobic tunnel of stalks. When he crested a swell, the world exploded outward again—vast, terrifyingly open, and dominated by the distant, jagged ivory of the White City.

The Anatomy of the Heat

By mid-afternoon, the "Effort" had taken a new, more insidious form.

On the mountain, the enemy was gravity and stone. Here, the enemy was the sun and the lack of a horizon. In the tall grass, Arin lost all sense of scale. Without the strider's crimson tail-feathers to follow, he would have been circling in his own tracks within the hour.

His skin, already wind-burned from the heights, began to crack under the relentless solar pressure. Every breath felt like inhaling warm silt. The water in his skin was being traded for the salt on his brow, and his tongue felt like a piece of dry leather forgotten in the dust.

Why am I following a bird? the doubt whispered, its voice dry and rasping. *What is a map with no landmarks? What is a city that never gets closer?*

He looked at his hands—the bandages were now stained with the yellow dust of the Veldt, the blood underneath itching as it healed into thick, ugly scars. These were no longer the hands of Arin Vale of Ellmere. They were the hands of a man who had carried a stranger down a mountain.

"I am not going back," he croaked, the words barely making it past his teeth. "The grass can have my bones, but it won't have my direction."

The Sign of the Navigator

As the sun began its long, slow lean toward the west, the strider stopped.

It didn't stop because it was tired. It stopped at a peculiar formation—three massive, black stones thrusting out of the amber waves like the fingers of a buried hand. They were obsidian, smooth and cool to the touch despite the heat.

Carved into the center stone, at exactly Arin's eye level, was a symbol.

It wasn't a word. It was a drawing of a compass, but instead of the four cardinal directions, it had seven. In the center of the compass was a small, indentation—the exact size of a human thumb.

Arin reached out. His thumb, calloused and stained, fit perfectly into the groove.

As he pressed, a low, mechanical hum vibrated through the stone. A small compartment slid open at the base of the pillar. Inside sat a flask of polished silver and a small, wax-sealed packet.

The Geometry of Hope

Arin drank. The water was cold—impossible, bone-deep cold—and tasted of mountain springs and mint. It wasn't just liquid; it was life. It flooded his senses, clearing the heat-fog from his brain and stilling the tremors in his legs.

He opened the packet. Inside were three small cakes of compressed grain and honey, and a single slip of paper.

The mountain tests the strength. The Veldt tests the faith. Keep the city on your left shoulder when the moon rises. The grass hides the path, but the stars hold the map. — **E.**

Arin looked at the strider. The bird let out a soft, rhythmic thrum and settled into the grass, tucking its head beneath a wing. It was done for the day.

The First Night in the Amber

Arin sat against the obsidian stone, the black rock radiating a gentle, stored warmth into his aching back. He pulled out his journal.

The light was turning a deep, bruised violet, the same color as the strider's eyes. For the first time, the "White City" didn't look like a ghost. With the sun behind it, Lumen cast a shadow that reached across the entire Veldt, a long, dark finger pointing directly at Arin.

He wrote, his pen moving with a newfound fluidity:

I have traded the vertical prison of the mountain for the horizontal maze of the grass. But the maze has bread. The maze has water. And for the first time, the maze has a name.

He looked up at the first stars blinking into existence.

Elias.

Whoever you are, you knew I was coming. You knew I would be thirsty. You knew I would be tempted to turn back. You are not a ghost, and you are not a memory. You are a destination.

Arin closed the book and watched the shadows swallow the gold. He wasn't afraid of the dark tonight. He was part of the map now.

(Part 6 — The Seven-Pointed Stars)

Arin sat with his back against the obsidian pillar, watching the transformation. In Ellmere, night was a curtain drawn over the day's chores. Here, night was an unveiling.

The sky above the Veldt was not the empty black he had known. It was crowded. A dense, glittering tapestry of stars spilled across the firmament, so bright they cast faint, sharp shadows of the grass against the black stone. But they were not the stars he had studied from his bedroom window.

He leaned forward, squinting. Above the distant silhouette of the White City, a specific constellation hung like a sigil: seven stars, arranged in a perfect, jagged heptagon. They didn't twinkle; they pulsed with a steady, rhythmic violet light that matched the eyes of the sleeping strider at his feet.

The Predators of the Grass

As the silence deepened, the "Effort" shifted again. It was no longer about movement; it was about stillness.

The Veldt at night was a theater of sound. He heard the low, guttural churr of insects the size of birds, and the distant, haunting cry of something that sounded like a woman laughing, miles away. Then came the *hush-hush* of the grass.

It wasn't the wind.

Something was moving through the stalks—something large, heavy, and methodical. It circled the obsidian pillar, staying just beyond the reach of the starlight. Arin's hand went to the notched paring knife. His breath caught in his throat, a sharp, cold lump.

Don't move, he told himself, the instinct of the mountain fox from the night before echoing in his blood. *In the grass, the one who moves is the one who is found.*

A pair of amber eyes, much larger than the fox's, ignited in the darkness twenty paces away. They were slit-pupiled and hungry. The creature let out a low, vibrating growl that he felt in the stone against his spine.

The strider didn't wake. It didn't even stir.

Arin realized then that the obsidian pillar wasn't just a marker; it was a sanctuary. The predator prowled the edge of an invisible line, its paws clicking against the hidden stones, but it did not cross. It was as if the "Seven-Pointed Compass" he had pressed earlier had activated a perimeter that the wild things of the Veldt knew better than to challenge.

The Internal Cartography

Arin let out a breath he felt he'd been holding since the river crossing. He reached for the journal, the silver light of the stars making the white pages glow like phosphorus.

He didn't write about the predator. He wrote about the geometry of the sky.

The stars in the valley were fragments, he wrote, his hand steady despite the cold. *But here, they are a language. There are seven points to the compass because there are seven ways to be lost, and only one way to be found.*

He looked at the map Elias had left him. In the starlight, he noticed a faint, shimmering thread of ink he hadn't seen in the sun. It was a secondary line, pulsing with the same violet hue as the heptagon above. It didn't lead to the city; it led to a point in the middle of the grass marked only by a small, silver flame.

The City is the goal, Arin realized, his mind racing. *But the Flame is the path.*

The Ghost of the Father

In the deep quiet of the watch, the "Psychological Impact" of the journey began to settle. He thought of his father—a man who had died in the same bed he was born in, his last words a complaint about the draft from the window.

His father would have hated this night. He would have been terrified of the amber eyes and the violet stars. He would have called the strider a demon and the obsidian pillar a tomb.

"You weren't afraid of the world, Father," Arin whispered into the cold air. "You were afraid of the scale of your own soul."

He realized then that the Ironcrest Mountains hadn't just been a physical barrier; they were a mercy for those who didn't want to see how vast the universe truly was. To live in Ellmere was to live in a thumbprint. To be here, under the seven-pointed stars, was to be a part of the design.

The Vigil of the Dawn

He didn't sleep much. He watched the stars rotate around the central violet point, a slow, celestial clock that made the Ellmere clocktower seem like a broken toy.

When the first gray light began to bleed into the eastern horizon, turning the silver grass back to dull bronze, the predator vanished. The amber eyes winked out, retreating into the deep troughs of the Veldt.

The strider stood up, shook its fire-colored feathers, and let out a sharp, bugling call that shattered the morning mist. It looked at Arin, its violet eyes expectant.

Arin stood, his body stiff but his mind a blade. He packed the silver flask—now refilled by some hidden mechanism in the stone—and the remnants of the honey-cakes.

He looked at the distant White City. It was no longer a ghost. It was a target.

"Today we find the flame," he said to the bird.

The strider turned and dove into the grass. Arin followed, his boots striking the earth with the confidence of a man who was no longer wandering, but being led.

(Part 7 — The Alchemist of the Amber)

The strider moved with a sudden, sharp purpose, its long neck dipping and weaving through the stalks like a needle through silk. Arin followed, his boots heavy with the yellow dust of the plains. The grass here was changing; it was no longer just amber, but streaked with veins of a deep, metallic blue—stalks that hummed when the wind brushed them, a low-frequency vibration that made the marrow of his bones itch.
Then, the grass simply stopped.

It didn't thin out. it ended in a perfect, scorched circle fifty paces wide. In the center of the circle sat a structure that defied the "Stillness" of Ellmere and the "Indifference" of the Ironcrests.

It was a wagon, but one built of the same white stone as the distant city, braced with ribs of copper that pulsed with a soft, rhythmic light. Atop the wagon sat a chimney that didn't exhale smoke, but a steady, translucent pillar of violet flame—the "Flame" from the map.

The Guardian of the Path

Standing beside a folding table cluttered with glass vials and brass instruments was a man.

He was not a "Giant." He was small, wiry, and dressed in robes the color of a thunderstorm. His hair was a wild shock of white, and his eyes, when he looked up, were not violet like the strider's, but a piercing, intelligent gray—the color of the mountain before the sun hits it.

"You're late," the man said. His voice wasn't a rasp; it was a crisp, melodic snap, like a dry twig breaking.

Arin stopped at the edge of the scorched earth. He felt the weight of his scarred hands, his ruined boots, and the salt-stained journal in his pack. "Late for what?"

"The crossing," the man said, gesturing to the shimmering horizon behind the wagon. "The Veldt doesn't stay gold forever, boy. The Season of the Scythe is coming. If you're still in the grass when the wind turns, you won't be a traveler. You'll be mulch."

The Alchemy of the Journey

The man stepped forward, his eyes scanning Arin with the intensity of a jeweler examining a raw stone. He reached out and grabbed Arin's hand—the one scarred from the mountain descent.

"Tomas told me you were stubborn," the man murmured, his thumb tracing the jagged line across Arin's palm.

Arin flinched. "You know Tomas?"

"I know everyone who tries the Ironcrests," the man said, releasing his hand. "My name is Elias. I am the Navigator of the Low Path. And you, Arin Vale, are the first person in three decades to carry someone *down* that mountain instead of stepping over them to reach the top."

He turned back to his table, picking up a vial of shimmering, iridescent liquid.

"The mountain was your test of strength," Elias continued, his back to Arin. "But the Veldt is a test of transformation. You think you are here to reach a city. You are not. You are here to become someone who is *allowed* to enter it."

The Price of the Map

Elias poured the liquid into a stone bowl. It hissed, releasing a scent of ozone and crushed jasmine.

"Lumen is not a place for the ghosts of the valley," Elias said, his voice dropping to a low, serious vibration. "It is a city of the 'Awake.' To enter, you must shed the last of your inherited skin. You must trade your memories for vision."

He held out the bowl. The liquid inside swirled with a seven-pointed star of light, mirroring the constellation from the night before.

"Drink," Elias commanded. "And tell me what you see when you look at the grass."

Arin hesitated. He thought of the baker's sign in Ellmere. He thought of the "Stillness." He realized that drinking from this bowl was the final act of treason against his old life. To drink was to admit that the world he knew was a lie.

He took the bowl. The stone was cold, vibrating with the same hum as the blue-veined grass.

He drank.

The Shattering of the Lens

The world didn't change, but Arin's perception of it exploded.

The amber grass was no longer just plants; it was a sea of data. He saw the currents of the wind as visible ribbons of silver. He saw the heat rising from the earth as a rhythmic pulse of crimson. And the White City—it was no longer a jagged silhouette. It was a beacon of pure, coherent light, singing a frequency that made his teeth ache.

But more than that, he saw himself.

He saw the "Stillness" of Ellmere clinging to him like a gray shroud, a heavy, dusty film of "shoulds" and "musts" that he had carried across the river and over the mountain.

With a roar of effort that came from his very soul, Arin reached out and *tore* the shroud.

The gray film evaporated into the violet flame of the wagon.

"There," Elias whispered, a small, knowing smile touching his lips. "Now the effort is real."

The New Entry

Arin fell to his knees, gasping. The world was too loud, too bright, too *alive*. He fumbled for his journal, his fingers finding the pages with a sensory precision he hadn't known existed.

He wrote, the ink appearing to glow on the paper:

The eyes I brought from the valley were blind. Elias has given me the sight of the mountain. I see the path now. It isn't a road. It's a rhythm. I am no longer walking toward the city. I am becoming the city.

He looked up at Elias. The Navigator was already packing his instruments, the white-stone wagon beginning to hum with a deep, gravitational power.

"The strider will take you to the gates," Elias said, climbing onto the driver's seat. "Don't look back, Arin. The valley is gone. The mountain is passed. The city is waiting to see if you can handle the light."

The violet flame flared, and the wagon began to move—not forward, but *through* the grass, the stalks parting in a wave of blue light.

Arin stood up. He felt light. He felt dangerous. He felt awake.

(Part 8 — The Threshold of Light)

The first sign of the Scythe was a silver line on the horizon, moving faster than a gallop. It wasn't a cloud; it was a wall of frost, a crystalline edge that was literally reaping the amber grass, turning the gold to brittle, translucent glass in its wake.
The strider let out a sharp, urgent bugle. It didn't wait. It bolted.

Arin ran.

In Ellmere, running was for children or for those fleeing a fire. Here, running was the only way to remain biological. If the frost caught him, he wouldn't just freeze; he would shatter.

His boots struck the earth with a rhythmic, percussive force. With his "Awake" vision, he didn't just see the ground; he saw the ley lines of the plateau—streaks of violet energy buried deep in the soil. He stepped only where the light was strongest, his body moving with a fluid, predatory grace that would have been unrecognizable to the man who had sat by the window in the valley.

The Anatomy of the Chase

The cold arrived first. It wasn't the damp chill of the mountain; it was a dry, vacuum-like cold that sucked the moisture from his lungs. Every breath was a shard of glass. Behind him, the sound of the Scythe was a continuous, high-pitched *tink-tink-tink*—the sound of a billion grass stalks freezing and collapsing into dust.

He didn't look back. He kept his eyes on the White City.

Lumen was no longer a destination; it was a furnace. The ivory towers were radiating a heat so intense it began to shimmer against the approaching frost. He was caught in the "Tension" the prompt demanded—squeezed between the absolute zero of the Veldt and the solar fire of the City.

"Faster," he hissed, his legs pumping, his heart a frantic, electric engine.

The strider was a streak of crimson fire ahead of him, its violet eyes fixed on the massive, seamless gates of the plateau. The bird wasn't just a guide; it was a bridge. It was carrying the frequency of the City, carving a path of warmth through the encroaching ice.

The Final Gate

The plateau rose abruptly from the grass—a vertical wall of polished white stone three hundred feet high. There were no stairs. There were no ladders.

There was only a single, vertical slit in the stone, glowing with the same seven-pointed light as the constellation.

The frost was ten paces behind him. He could feel the hairs on his neck turning to ice. The silver line of the Scythe hit the base of the plateau, and the world behind Arin simply... broke. The sound was deafening, a tectonic scream of shattered crystal.

Arin leapt.

He didn't jump for a ledge; he jumped for the light.

As he crossed the threshold of the slit, the cold vanished instantly. It was replaced by a silence so profound it felt like being underwater. He tumbled onto a floor of smooth, warm alabaster, his lungs heaving, his skin stinging from the rapid transition.

The Entry in the Hall of Mirrors

He lay there for a long time, the strider standing over him, its violet eyes reflecting a world of impossible geometry.

Arin sat up. He was inside the gatehouse of Lumen. The walls weren't stone; they were memory. They were translucent, and as he moved, he saw reflections of himself—not the Arin of the valley, or the Arin of the mountain, but a thousand versions of the man he was *becoming*.

He pulled the journal from his pack. It was the only thing from the "Old World" that still felt real. He opened it to the very last page of Chapter 2.

The paper was no longer white; it had taken on a faint, pearlescent sheen. He took his pen—the nib now worn down to a blunt, powerful point—and wrote the final lines of the effort.

The Scythe has taken the grass, he wrote. *The mountain has taken the man. But the City has taken the soul. I am standing in the light that Ellmere feared. It does not burn. It reveals.*

He looked at his hands. The scars were still there, but they were glowing with a faint, internal silver. They were no longer wounds; they were his credentials.

Effort is not a ladder, he concluded. *It is a fire. And I am finally, truly, consumed.*

The End of the Beginning

The inner gates of Lumen began to spiral open—not outward, but inward, like the iris of a giant eye. Beyond lay the White City, a labyrinth of glass, water, and light, where the "Giants" waited to see what the man from the valley had brought them.

Arin stood. He didn't look back at the frost-covered waste. He didn't think of the baker or the clocktower.

He walked into the light.

Chapter 2 was over. The World was just beginning.

CHAPTER 3 - THE STORM THAT CHOOSES

(Part 1 — The Living Deep)

The western coast did not arrive gently. It did not offer a gradual transition of sand and tide. It revealed itself as a colossal fracture in the world, where the solid certainty of the earth simply surrendered to the infinite.

Arin heard it long before the first salt-spray touched his skin. It was a sound that didn't enter through the ears, but through the soles of his boots—a deep, tectonic roar that vibrated in his very marrow. It was the sound of something alive, immeasurable, and ancient. It rolled across the headlands in long, breathing waves of percussion, rising and falling with a rhythm that made the Ellmere clocktower seem like a heartbeat in a flea.

Then—the horizon broke open.

The ocean stretched before him, a sapphire desert that refused to stay still. It was nothing like the stagnant peace of the valley. It was nothing like the Ironcrest Mountains. Those had been statues of stone, demanding effort to conquer their silence. But this—this was a liquid engine. It was restless, uncontained, and violently alive.

Arin stood at the edge of the world, the wind forcing the scent of salt, kelp, and distance into his lungs. Below him, waves the size of houses slammed into jagged obsidian rocks, exploding into plumes of white foam that looked like the breath of a dying god. There was no hesitation in the water. No stillness.

In Ellmere, everything waited for permission. The ocean waited for nothing.

The Virella: A Splinter in the Infinite

By dusk, the scale of the coast had forced a new kind of humility upon him. He had found passage on a trading vessel named *The Virella*.

To his valley-born eyes, she looked impossibly fragile—a splinter of oak and hemp held together by prayer and pitch. She was not grand; she was scarred. Her wooden planks were worn smooth by decades of salt-friction, and her ropes hung coiled like sleeping serpents in the shadows of the gunwales. Her sails were a mosaic of patches, a history of storms survived stitched into every yard of canvas.

The crew moved with a terrifying, practiced urgency. There was no idle thought here. Every knot tied was a contract with survival. They understood the one truth Arin was only beginning to sense: the sea does not forgive. It only forgets.

“You’ve got the look of someone who hasn’t met the ocean yet.”

The voice was like a low-frequency hum. Arin turned to find the Captain—a man whose face looked as if it had been carved from driftwood and cured in brine. His eyes were the color of a winter squall, sharp enough to see through the fog of a man's intentions.

“I’ve seen it,” Arin replied, gesturing to the crashing surf.

The Captain gave a faint, haunting smile. It wasn't a smile of kindness; it was a smile of perspective. “No,” he said softly. “You’ve seen the surface. You’ve seen the mask the deep wears when it wants you to step aboard.”

The Descent into the Black

They set sail as the sun surrendered to the waves. The shoreline—the last tether to the world of dirt and stone—faded with a brutal finality. Soon, there was no "Out," no "Valley," and no "Mountain." There was only the *Virella*, a tiny bubble of lantern-light in an ocean of absolute black.

At first, the sea was a liar.

It was calm. Too calm. The ship glided across the surface with an eerie, velvet ease. The water whispered against the hull, a soft, seductive sound like silk tearing. Even the Captain seemed to relax, his hand resting lightly on the tiller.

Arin stood at the rail, looking down into the void. It felt like standing on the edge of a god's eye. The water was a mirror that reflected nothing, a space so infinite it threatened to erase his very name.

The mountain was a test of my legs, he thought, his fingers gripping the cold wood of the railing. *The forest was a test of my hunger. But this... this is a test of my presence.*

The Eruption of the Heavens

By midnight, the sky decided that the silence had lasted long enough.

It did not build. It did not warn. It erupted.

Thunder cracked with a sound so violent Arin felt his teeth ache. It wasn't a roll; it was a fracture—the sky itself breaking under the weight of its own shadows. A blinding flash of lightning tore through the dark, illuminating the world in a strobe-light of silver horror.

And in that instant, Arin saw the truth the Captain had promised.

The waves were no longer waves. They were walls. Moving mountains of water, emerald-black and crested with jagged foam, rising high above the masts. They didn't flow; they marched with a terrifying, rhythmic purpose.

"STORM!" a voice screamed, but the wind caught the word and shredded it before it could reach the bow.

"REEF THE SAILS! MOVE! MOVE!"

The *Virella* lurched. The deck tilted at an impossible angle, throwing Arin sideways. He slammed into the railing, his boots sliding on the sudden deluge of freezing saltwater. The ocean had dropped the mask. It wasn't hostile; it was simply being itself. And what it was, was a force that didn't recognize the existence of men.

The wind howled, but it wasn't the sound of air moving. It was a high-pitched, predatory scream—the sound of the void realizing it had something to crush.

(Part 2 — The Iron Grip of the Void)

The Virella was no longer a ship; it was a drum being beaten by the fists of a god. Every time the hull slammed into the trough of a wave, the sound was a sickening, structural groan that Arin felt in his teeth. It was the sound of wood reaching its limit. Saltwater, as cold as the glacial run-off of the Ironcrests, swept across the deck in waist-high surges, threatening to peel the men from the wood like dead scales.

"HOLD THE LINE!" a sailor screamed, his face a mask of streaming brine and terror.

He thrust a thick, salt-crusted hemp rope into Arin's hands. The friction was instantaneous—a searing, abrasive heat that tore through the callouses he had earned on the mountain. The rope wasn't just heavy; it was alive. It bucked and pulled with the strength of the gale, trying to drag Arin toward the churning white madness of the gunwales.

The Anatomy of Paralysis

Lightning split the sky again, a jagged vein of violet fire that turned the world into a silver photograph for a heartbeat.

And in that flash, Arin saw him.

A boy. He couldn't have been more than seventeen—the age Arin had been when he first started dreaming of the world beyond the well. He was standing beside the mainmast, his hands hovering inches from a belaying pin, his fingers curled into useless, trembling talons.

He wasn't moving. He wasn't even blinking.

The boy was experiencing the "Stillness" of Ellmere, but in its most lethal form. It was the paralysis of a mind that had finally met a reality it couldn't categorize. The roar of the ocean had reached a frequency that had simply turned his soul to glass.

"MOVE!" someone bellowed, a shadow of a man rushing past to secure a flapping jib.

But the boy was gone. He was a statue of salt and fear.

The Fractal Choice

Arin looked at the rope in his own hands. His muscles were screaming, his shoulders feeling as if they were being pulled from their sockets. If he let go to reach the boy, the line would snap back, likely maiming the sailor next to him. If he stayed, the boy would be swept overboard by the next mountain of water currently rising over the port bow.

Time didn't slow down; it fractured.

He saw the mountain. He saw the "Choice" he had made with Tomas. But this wasn't a slow crawl down a cliff. This was a decision made in the strobe-light of a hurricane.

Choice defines who you become.

The words from his journal didn't feel like philosophy anymore. They felt like a command. He wasn't a passenger on the *Virella*. He wasn't a passenger in his own life.

“TAKE THE WEIGHT!” Arin roared at the sailor behind him, shoving the slack of the rope into the man’s startled grip.

The Sprint through the Chasm

Arin ran.

The deck pitched at a forty-five-degree angle. He didn't run with his legs; he ran with his center of gravity, sliding across the slick, heaving planks. A wave crashed over the side, a literal ton of ocean slamming into his side, nearly throwing him into the dark.

He caught himself on a brass cleat, his knuckles screaming, and lunged for the mast.

He grabbed the boy’s shoulders. They were as hard as stone.

“HEY!” Arin shouted, his face inches from the boy’s. “LOOK AT ME!”

The boy’s eyes flickered. They were wide, the pupils blown so large they looked like ink-wells. He wasn't seeing the storm; he was seeing his own death.

“I—I can’t—” the boy stammered, the words lost in the scream of the wind.

“You can,” Arin said. He didn't use the voice of a clerk or a traveler. He used the voice of the man who had looked the Ironcrests in the eye and refused to blink. “You just haven’t yet. GRAB THE LINE!”

The Union of the Effort

Another wave hit. The ship groaned, a terrifying *crack* echoing from somewhere deep in the hold. The mainmast shuddered, the sail above them snapping with the sound of a giant’s whip. If that sail tore free, it wouldn't just be lost; it would take the rigging with it. It would turn the *Virella* into a drifting coffin.

“HELP ME!” Arin yelled, his hands finding the freezing, thrashing rope of the mainsail.

Something shifted in the boy. It wasn't courage—not the heroic kind found in poems. it was the raw, electric necessity of the "Awake." He reached out. His fingers found the hemp.

Together, they pulled.

The force was brutal. It was as if they were trying to wrestle a dragon made of wind. The rope burned through Arin's palms, the salt stinging the fresh raw skin, but he didn't feel the pain. He felt the weight. He felt the connection.

He wasn't just saving a ship. He was anchoring a soul.

“PULL!”

(Part 3 — The Eye of the Revelation)

The world turned white.

It wasn't the white of snow or the white of the city; it was the blinding, electric white of a sky that had forgotten how to be dark. A mountain of water, larger than any that had preceded it, rose over the starboard side. It didn't just crash; it fell.

"HOLD!" Arin screamed, his voice a rasping tear in the wind.

He didn't grab the railing. He grabbed the boy. He wrapped his arm around the mast and his other around the kid's chest, anchoring them both to the spine of the ship. The impact was a physical concussion. A ton of freezing, aerated salt-water slammed into them, trying to peel their skin from their bones, trying to fill their lungs with the weight of the deep.

For five seconds, Arin was underwater while standing on a deck. There was no air. There was only the roar of the abyss.

Then, the ship rose.

The *Virella* shuddered, water cascading off the deck in a series of drowning waterfalls. Arin gasped, coughing up brine, his vision spotting with black. But the line—the one he and the boy had fought for—was secure. The mainsail was reefed. The mast had held.

The Aftermath of the Force

Slowly, the violence of the sky began to retreat. It didn't fade into a drizzle; it simply pulled back, like a predator that had grown bored of its prey. The thunder moved from a crack to a distant, surly growl. The lightning stopped its strobe-light interrogation, leaving only a bruised, purple twilight behind.

The waves lowered from mountains to hills, then to a restless, undulating motion.

Silence fell. Not the artificial, suffocating "Stillness" of Ellmere. Not the pressurized silence of the Ironcrests. This was a silence earned through the friction of bone against hemp. It was the silence of survivors.

Arin stood on the deck, his body vibrating with a fatigue so deep it felt like his blood had turned to lead. His clothes were shredded, his boots filled with water, and his hands—the hands that had once held only a clerk's pen—were raw, bloody, and beautiful.

The boy stood beside him. He wasn't the statue of salt anymore. He was breathing. He looked at his own hands, then up at Arin. There were no words, but in the gray light of the dawn, his eyes held a new, hard clarity. He was no longer seventeen. He was "Awake."

The Captain's Mark

The Captain approached through the wreckage of the deck—shattered crates, tangled rope, and the smell of ozone. He didn't look at the sky. He looked at the mast. He looked at the knot Arin and the boy had tied together.

He stepped forward and placed a hand on Arin's shoulder. It was a heavy, calloused weight—a seal of brotherhood.

"You saved this vessel," the Captain said. His voice was steady, but it carried the vibration of the storm.

Arin looked out at the horizon. The sun was beginning to bleed over the edge of the world, a soft, golden line that turned the predatory ocean into a field of shimmering diamonds. It looked peaceful. It looked like a lie.

"No," Arin said quietly.

The Captain tilted his head, a question in his gray eyes.

"The ocean didn't care about the ship," Arin continued, his voice finding its strength. "The storm didn't choose to let us live. We chose to stay on the deck. We chose to pull."

He realized then that the "Stillness" of his old life wasn't just a lack of movement. It was a lack of choice. In Ellmere, life happened *to* you. Here, life was something you wrestled from the wind.

The Final Line

Arin reached into his wet pack. The journal was damp, the leather smelling of salt and old leather, but the pages were intact. He found a dry spot near the back.

The morning breeze caught the paper, flipping through his history—the forest, the mountain, the fox, the city. He looked at the boy, who was now helping a sailor clear the debris. He looked at the horizon.

He wrote, the ink bleeding slightly into the damp paper, creating a permanent, blurred shadow:

In calm, we imagine who we are. We build monuments to our intentions and altars to our dreams.

He paused, the sun hitting the page.

In chaos, we become it. The storm didn't change me. it just stripped away the man I was pretending to be until only the truth was left. I am not a traveler. I am a choice.

He closed the journal.

The *Virella* turned its bow toward the south, toward the next horizon, toward the next mystery. Arin Vale stood at the rail, his face turned toward the spray. He wasn't waiting for the world to move him anymore.

He was the motion.

CHAPTER 4 - THE CITY OF EASY CHOICES

(Part 1 — The Architecture of Narcissism)

The city did not appear; it unfolded like the petals of a predatory flower. Arin first saw it from the crest of a low ridge just beyond the coast road—a shimmer of light where there should have been the haze of distance. At first, he thought it was a mirage, the sun reflecting off the salt-rimed sea. But the shape held. It expanded. It breathed with a soft, rhythmic luminescence that made the air around it feel charged with static.

Then—it revealed itself.

Aurelia. A city of impossible, geometric grace.

White stone towers rose like sculpted pillars of frozen light, their surfaces polished so fine they didn't just reflect the sun—they seemed to amplify it into a soft, pearl-colored brilliance. Wide avenues curved with deliberate elegance, lined with trees whose leaves were not green, but a translucent, glass-like silver that chimed in the breeze. Balconies overflowed with flora that defied the season: deep crimson vines, gold-veined violets, and blue lilies that hummed at a frequency that vibrated in Arin's jaw.

Everything about Aurelia felt intentional. Every stone was placed to please the eye; every fountain was tuned to soothe the ear. It was a masterpiece of urban design, a utopia carved from the chaos of the coast.

Arin stood at the ridge longer than he meant to. He didn't feel the awe that had struck him at the mountains or the terror of the sea. He felt a strange, cooling hesitation.

Because beneath the beauty, there was a void. It didn't call to him like a challenge; it welcomed him like a bed. And that, he would later realize, was a far more lethal threat.

The Softening of the World

By the time he passed through the high, arched gates, the world had fundamentally softened.

The air was warmer here, scented with vanilla and crushed jasmine, lacking the sharp, metallic bite of the ocean spray. Even the sounds of the city—the rhythmic tap of sandals on marble, the murmurs of conversation, the distant, liquid notes of a harp—flowed together into a carefully composed melody.

There were no sharp edges in Aurelia. No urgency. No struggle.

"First time?" a voice asked.

Arin turned. A man stood nearby, draped in tailored linen that looked as if it had never known dust. His expression was easy, his eyes bright with a superficial kind of peace.

“It shows,” the man added, his smile perfect and practiced. “You’re still looking for the friction. You’re still tensed for the climb.”

“Is that unusual?” Arin asked, his voice sounding rough, even to his own ears.

The man chuckled, a sound like silver coins falling into velvet. “Only at the beginning. Soon, you’ll realize the mountain is just a story we tell to scare children. Here, the only direction is *forward*.”

The Economy of Ease

The streets were alive, but it was a choreographed life. Merchants displayed goods that seemed too refined for human hands—silks that moved like running water, glass that bent light into colors that didn't exist in the valley, and food that carried aromas so rich they triggered memories Arin didn't even own.

And money—money flowed like a silent, underground river.

“You work?” the man asked casually as they walked toward a plaza of shimmering fountains.

“I travel,” Arin replied, his hand instinctively touching the worn strap of his pack.

The man nodded as if Arin had said something profoundly obvious. “Well,” he said, gesturing to the gilded paradise around them, “here, those are the same thing. To experience Aurelia is to earn it. The city provides for those who appreciate the view.”

Arin didn't understand the price then. He only saw the reward.

The first coin came with a terrifying ease. A merchant asked him to help move three small crates of "essence" from one end of the market to another. The crates were light, smelling of summer rain. The pay was a gold leaf—a week’s wages in the valley for ten minutes of walking.

The second coin was easier. The third was a gift for simply "suggesting" a color for a noble's new cloak.

By the end of the first week, the unusual had become the expected. The "Effort" was being replaced by "Flow."

The Erasure of the Soul

Days bled into weeks, and the sharpness of Arin's intent began to dull.

He found himself settling into rhythms he had never intended to create. His mornings, once dictated by the rising sun and the necessity of miles, now came later, cushioned by silk sheets and the soft, ambient music of the city. His meals were no longer fuel; they were experiences. His rooms offered a softness he hadn't known since his mother's house in Ellmere—but without its weight, without its suffocating "Stillness."

Aurelia was designed to remove friction. It smoothed the edges of a man's life until nothing resisted. Nothing challenged. Nothing demanded more than he was willing to give.

And so—without realizing the trade he was making—Arin began to give less.

His steps grew slower. His thoughts grew quieter. The fierce, electric clarity he had found in the storm was being drowned in a sea of honeyed comfort.

The journal stayed in the bottom of his bag.

At first, the absence of his pen felt like a phantom limb—a sharp, phantom ache. But the city had a way of filling every silence with a distraction, every reflection with a new sensation.

“Why think so much?” a woman laughed one evening, her eyes reflecting the golden lanterns of a floating café. “Life isn't a problem to be solved, Arin. It’s a vintage to be tasted.”

And for a long, golden month, Arin Vale believed her. He smiled easily. He laughed effortlessly. He drifted through the white stone towers like a ghost in a palace of light.

He was happy. And that was the most dangerous thing he had ever been.

(Part 2 — The Silence of the Unwritten)

The days in Aurelia did not pass; they dissolved. Time here was not a river with a current; it was a still, shallow pool reflecting a permanent noon.

Arin sat in a quiet corner of the *Café of the Sun*, a balcony suspended over a plaza of dancing water. A cup of spiced nectar rested untouched in his hand, the steam rising in a lazy, fragrant spiral. He wasn't tired. He wasn't unhappy. He wasn't even restless.

And that—as a single, stray thought pierced the honeyed fog of his mind—was the problem.

He searched himself for the "Vibration." He looked for the electric hum he had felt in the Ironcrests, the jagged urgency of the storm, the violet pulse of the "Awake" vision Elias had given him.

There was nothing.

Only a profound, terrifying comfort. He was a stone at the bottom of a well, perfectly settled, perfectly safe, and utterly motionless.

The Weight of the Absence

His hand moved to his bag. It felt lighter than it should. The leather was supple now, cleaned of the mountain dust and the sea salt by a servant he hadn't even asked to help.

He opened it.

The journal lay at the bottom, tucked beneath a silk scarf and a bag of gold leaves. He pulled it out. It didn't feel like a living thing anymore. It felt like a relic from a different life—a heavy, accusatory block of wood.

He opened the cover.

The first page: Today I begin. The second: Not every path forward leads upward. The third: In calm, we imagine who we are. In chaos, we become it.

And then—a desert of white.

Arin flipped through the pages. One. Five. Ten. Twenty. Blank. Blank. Blank. The paper was pristine, lacking even a smudge of ink or a drop of sweat. It was a record of a month spent in the "Stillness" he thought he had escaped.

A quiet realization settled over him, cold as a mountain shadow. He had not written in weeks. Not because he was too busy, but because there had been nothing worth the ink. Nothing had demanded his strength. Nothing had challenged his ethics. Nothing had forced him to choose between his safety and his soul.

Aurelia had given him everything—and taken his story in return.

The Cage of Ease

He looked up at the café. The people around him were beautiful, their laughter melodic, their lives seemingly perfect. But as the alchemical "sight" from the Veldt flickered back to life, he saw them differently.

They weren't "Awake." They were dreaming.

The city was a masterpiece of anesthesia. It was a prison without bars, a cage made of "Yes." It was a place where you could spend eighty years and never once find out who you were, because you were never once required to be anything but comfortable.

"Comfort is the most beautiful prison ever built," Arin whispered.

The words felt like a physical strike. He grabbed his pen—the nib dry, the ink clotted—and forced it onto the page. He wrote the line with a jagged, violent energy, the ink tearing into the expensive paper.

The illusion is broken, he added beneath it. *I am being erased by pleasure. I am being murdered by a lack of friction.*

The Break-Out

That night, he did not go to the theater of floating lights. He did not attend the feast of the merchant lords.

He went to his room—a chamber of marble and silk—and began to pack. He threw away the tailored linens. He discarded the gold leaves, leaving them scattered across the polished floor like fallen autumn debris. He put back on his old wool tunic, now patched and smelling of cedar, and cinched his belt tight.

The room, which had felt like a sanctuary an hour ago, now felt like a tomb.

Sleep did not come. He sat by the window, watching the city's lanterns glow with a predatory beauty. He realized that Aurelia didn't need guards at the gates. It didn't need walls. It simply waited for the traveler to forget why they were traveling.

Many never left. They stayed until their journals were forgotten, until their "Effort" became a myth, until they were just another reflection in the white stone towers.

The Threshold of the Gate

Morning arrived with its usual, deceptive peace. The sun turned the towers to pearl. The silver trees chimed their morning greeting.

Arin stepped onto the street. He walked toward the high, arched gates, his pack heavy once more, his boots striking the marble with a sound of discordance. The people he passed looked at him with a faint, pitying confusion. Why would anyone leave the "Easy Choice" for the "Hard Road"?

At the threshold, he paused. He looked back at the shimmering spires of Aurelia.

It would continue without him. It would find new travelers to soften, new stories to silence. It was a perfect world, and Arin Vale realized he no longer wanted to live in a world that was finished. He wanted to live in a world that was being built.

He turned his back on the white stone.

The road ahead was dusty, rutted, and disappeared into a forest of dark, tangled thorns. It looked uncomfortable. It looked dangerous.

Arin took a breath, the air tasting of earth and effort once more.

"I am Awake," he murmured.

He took his next step. Not toward the light of the city, but toward the shadow of the unknown. Behind him, the gates of Aurelia remained wide open—the most terrifying invitation he had ever survived.

CHAPTER 5 - THE DESERT OF SILENCE

(Part 1 — The Great Erasure)

The desert did not begin. It erased.

One moment, there was a road—a tangible thread of gravel and dust that promised a destination. There was a direction, a sense of momentum, the lingering scent of the coastal salt. And then—as if a god had simply wiped a damp cloth across the map—there was nothing.

The land flattened into a terrifying infinity of pale gold and bone-white, stretching beyond the reach of sight, beyond the grasp of reason. There were no trees to measure the wind. No structures to break the horizon. No markers to prove that Arin was moving at all. It was just sand—layer upon shifting layer of it—breathing with an ancient, tectonic indifference.

The sky above it was too wide. It was a vault of relentless blue that felt less like an atmosphere and more like an interrogation. It was too open. Too honest. It offered no shadows to hide in, no clouds to soften the glare. It simply watched.

Arin stepped forward, and the silence hit him like a physical blow.

The ground shifted beneath him, a soft, unstable powder that swallowed the edges of his boots with every step. The wind moved across the dunes in long, whispering strokes, reshaping the world in real-time. It was a place that refused to be remembered. Nothing stayed. No footprint survived for more than a minute.

He turned once, an instinctive reflex born of a lifetime of looking back.

The path behind him was gone. Not faded. Not distant. It was as if the earth had healed over behind his heels, leaving him stranded in a permanent Now.

A cold, sharp sensation crept into his chest. It wasn't fear—not the jagged, electric fear of the storm. It was something heavier. Something clinical. For the first time since he had closed the door to his house in Ellmere, there was no way back. The desert hadn't closed a door; it had deleted the house.

The Pressure of the Void

The first day passed with a grueling, rhythmic quiet.

The sun did not burn; it pressed. It was a constant, atmospheric weight that drained the moisture from his skin and the energy from his marrow. It didn't attack in bursts; it conducted a slow, steady harvest.

There were no sounds. No birds to cry out, no insects to hum, not even the rustle of dry brush. There was only the sound of his own pulse, thumping like a muffled drum in his ears, and the dry hiss of sand against leather.

He tried to focus on his progress. He counted his steps. He timed his breaths. But without landmarks, time began to loosen its grip. It warped. It stretched thin until an hour felt like a frantic minute, then curled back until a single minute felt like a decade of exposure.

By nightfall, the desert revealed its second face. The heat vanished with a suddenness that made his bones ache. It was replaced by a cold that felt personal—a predatory chill that sought out the warmth in his blood and tried to extinguish it.

Arin collapsed onto the sand, his body a map of exhaustion. He looked up, and the sky opened.

The Intrusive Infinite

In Ellmere, the stars were a ceiling—contained, familiar, and framed by the silhouettes of trees. Here, they were a flood.

Millions of them burned with a terrifying, impossible clarity, filling the sky so completely that the darkness itself seemed to have been shredded. They didn't feel distant; they felt like they were pressing down on him, millions of cold, bright eyes witnessing his smallness.

Alone.

The word didn't arrive as a thought. It arrived as a tectonic realization. It wasn't a temporary situation; it was a fundamental truth. Beneath this sky, on this sand, he wasn't Arin the Traveler or Arin the Hero. He was a single, flickering spark in a cold, infinite room.

The Interior Harvest

The second day stripped away the last of his distractions.

His pace slowed, not because the sand was deeper, but because the absence was heavier. With nothing to look at, nothing to anticipate, and no one to speak to, his mind began to fill the vacuum. It was a survival mechanism gone wrong.

At first, it was fragments—the smell of the bakery in Ellmere, the sound of a closing gate, the taste of a cold apple. But as the sun pressed harder, the memories turned into ghosts.

Regrets surfaced. Not the loud, dramatic kind, but the quiet, persistent ones. Moments where he had chosen the "Easy Choice" over the "Right Truth." Silence where he should have spoken. Comfort where he should have grown. They didn't accuse him with screams; they simply sat beside him in the sand, waiting for him to acknowledge them.

The desert did not chase him. It didn't need to. It just waited for him to run out of places to hide from himself.

By the third day, the Doubt arrived. It had a voice—his own voice, but stripped of hope.

“Why are you doing this?” it whispered through the heat-haze. “What are you actually searching for? Is the journey real, or are you just a man walking in a circle until he dies?”

Arin stopped. The horizon was a flat, shimmering line of nothing. He looked at his hands, scarred from the mountain and the sea, and for the first time, they felt like they belonged to a stranger.

Fear finally arrived. Not fear of the heat or the cold, but fear of the person standing in his boots. Because in the Desert of Silence, there is nowhere left to look except inward.

(Part 2 — The Internal Siege)

By the third afternoon, the desert had finished with his body and began to dismantle his mind.

The heat-haze on the horizon didn't just shimmer; it hallucinated. He saw the Iron-crests rising from the sand, cold and jagged, only to dissolve into the white towers of Aurelia as he blinked. The memories weren't just thoughts anymore; they were projections on the pale gold canvas of the dunes.

"You're still walking," the voice said. It was his own voice, but it sounded like it was coming from the sand beneath his feet. "But you aren't moving. You're just vibrating in place while the world turns around you."

Arin didn't answer. His throat was a dry canyon, his tongue a heavy, useless stone.

"Why did you leave the city?" the voice pressed, sharper now, like a needle. "The comfort was real. The gold was real. This? This is just a slow suicide for the sake of a journal no one will ever read."

The Geometry of Fear

Arin stopped. He looked at his shadow, which had grown long and skeletal in the dying light. It looked like a stranger—a jagged, dark shape that didn't belong in this perfect, empty world.

For the first time, fear arrived. Not the electric fear of a storm or the physical fear of a fall, but a deep, existential horror. He was afraid of the person standing in his boots because that person had no answers.

He sank to his knees. The sand shifted, unstable and unanchored, mirroring the collapse of his certainty.

"You left Ellmere for this?" the voice hissed. "You turned away from the mountain... for a grave made of dust?"

Each question struck with the weight of a hammer. He searched for a defense, a reason, a grand purpose. He reached for the "Awake" vision Elias had given him, but the desert was too honest for magic. It showed him exactly what he was: a man, alone, with a book of half-finished thoughts.

And suddenly—that didn't feel like enough.

The Alchemy of the Night

Night hit the desert like a shutter closing.

The stars returned, more intrusive than before, millions of cold, white fires that seemed to be drawing the heat directly out of his skin. Arin lay on his back, staring into the infinite. They didn't comfort him. They exposed him.

With no noise, no people, and no movement, there was only the raw, messy truth of his own life. It wasn't clean. It wasn't a hero's journey. It was a series of stumbles, a collection of moments where he had been brave and moments where he had been a coward.

The silence pressed in, heavy and unavoidable. And then—something shifted.

The voice stopped asking. It stopped mocking.

And Arin—for the first time in his life—started listening. Not to the questions, but to the space *beneath* them. The quiet beneath the doubt. The truth beneath the noise.

In that stillness, something surfaced. Not a revelation from a god, but a realization from a man. He had been moving forward, but he hadn't been looking. He had been testing his strength against mountains and seas, but he hadn't tested his honesty against himself.

The Most Permanent Line

Arin sat up slowly. The cold air moved around him, sharp and grounding. He didn't feel stronger, but he felt *clearer*. The desert hadn't given him a map; it had stripped away the blindfold.

He reached into his bag and pulled out the journal. The leather felt different now—not like a burden, but like an anchor. He opened it to a fresh page, the paper glowing pale in the starlight.

He didn't write about the heat. He didn't write about the sand. He wrote about the silence.

Most people fear silence, he wrote, his hand steady even in the chill, *because it forces them to read their own lives honestly. It is the only mirror that cannot be blurred by movement.*

He looked at the words. They felt heavier than any he had written before. They weren't a description of a journey; they were the result of one.

He closed the journal. And for the first time since entering the waste, the silence no longer felt like an enemy. It felt like space. Not empty, but clear.

The Departure from the Void

The next morning, the desert remained unchanged. It was still endless. It was still indifferent.

But Arin was not.

He stood up, adjusted his pack, and took a step forward. He didn't walk faster, but he walked with a new, quiet precision. He no longer needed a landmark to know he was moving. He was the landmark.

The desert did not end that day, or the next. But it no longer needed to. Its lesson had already been written—not in the sand, where the wind could erase it, but in the marrow of his bones.

He looked toward the horizon, where a new shape was beginning to form through the haze—something dark, jagged, and solid.

The silence had done its work. Now, it was time for the noise to begin again.

CHAPTER 6 - THE BRIDGE OF NO RETURN

(Part 1 — The Green Choke)

The jungle did not open. It closed.

Arin did not see the moment he crossed the threshold from the arid waste into the emerald deep. He felt it. The transition was a physical weight, a sudden atmospheric shift that suggested the world had grown denser, more territorial.

The air thickened first—heavy, wet, and aggressively alive. It clung to his skin like a damp shroud and slid into his lungs with a cloying sweetness of rot and nectar. Sunlight, which had been a blunt instrument in the desert, was now fractured into jagged, shifting shards of green and gold. It fought its way through a canopy so thick it seemed to drink the day itself, leaving the forest floor in a permanent, humid twilight.

Then, the sound returned.

In the desert, silence had been a mirror. Here, sound was a weapon. A distant, prehistoric cry tore through the trees; a rustle in the undergrowth snapped shut the moment he turned his head. The low, electric hum of billions of unseen insects vibrated in his teeth.

Every step Arin took was a trespass. Every pause revealed a thousand eyes watching from the shadows of broad, gold-veined leaves. The jungle wasn't just a place; it was a breathing, hungry secret.

The Wound in the Earth

Time in the Green Choke was not measured in miles, but in awareness. Hours dissolved into a singular, focused effort to navigate a floor of twisted roots that coiled like petrified serpents beneath the damp mulch.

Then, the acoustic landscape shifted. A new sound emerged—a low-frequency thrum that drowned out the insect hum. It was a rhythmic, tectonic roar.

Water.

Arin moved toward it, the vegetation thickening until the path was a mere suggestion. He hacked through a wall of hanging vines, and suddenly, the world simply... ended.

The earth dropped away into a colossal canyon, a jagged vertical wound that looked as if a titan had struck the crust with an axe. Hundreds of feet below, a river didn't flow—it warred. It collided with obsidian boulders, exploding into plumes of white fury and mist that rose like ghosts. The sound was no longer heard; it was felt, a violent vibration that rattled Arin's ribcage and made the very ledge beneath his boots tremble.

The Thread over the Abyss

The canyon was too wide to jump, the walls too sheer to climb. There was only the Bridge.

It was a nightmare of frayed hemp and silvered wood, suspended over the churning white chaos like a fragile, dying thought. The ropes sagged under their own ancient weight, the fibers weeping dust with every gust of wind. Planks were missing, leaving gaping maws that looked down into the three-hundred-foot drop. It swayed with a slow, sickening rhythm, even without a traveler.

It didn't promise a crossing. It offered a gamble.

Arin looked back at the jungle—the suffocating, emerald maze. Then he looked ahead. He realized that some paths aren't meant to be walked; they are meant to be survived.

He stepped onto the first plank.

The bridge shrieked. It was a high-pitched, structural groan of rusted iron and snapping fiber. The ropes tightened, vibrating with a tension that felt like a scream held behind teeth. Arin froze. The canyon roared beneath him, a hungry, mindless mouth.

Step. Pause. Balance.

He moved with agonizing precision. He could see the individual strands of the handrail unspooling under his grip. The wind buffeted him, trying to tip his center of gravity into the void. The bridge stretched, lengthening the distance as fear began to warp his perception of space.

The Snap of Certainty

He reached the midpoint, suspended over the very heart of the white-water fury.

CRACK.

It wasn't a small sound. It was the report of a rifle. A primary support cable, eaten through by decades of jungle rot, snapped. The bridge didn't just shake; it buckled. The entire structure dipped violently to the left, the deck becoming a slide of slick, mossy wood.

Arin dropped to his knees, his fingers clawing into the fraying hemp as he dangled over the abyss.

Snap. Snap. Snap.

The sound of cascading failure followed. Planks splintered and fell, spinning like matchsticks into the roar below. He looked back—the section behind him was already disintegrating, falling into the mists.

There was no retreat. The "Return" was being deleted in real-time.

"Forward," he gritted out, the word tasting of copper and adrenaline.

He didn't walk. He didn't crawl. He ignited.

Arin lunged forward just as the second cable gave way. The bridge was no longer a path; it was a falling staircase. He ran as the wood crumbled beneath his boots, leaping over gaps that grew wider with every heartbeat. The world narrowed to a single, white-hot line of survival.

Step. Break. Step. Snap.

The far ledge was a blur of red earth and solid roots. With a final, desperate roar of effort, Arin launched himself into the air as the last anchor point sheared off the stone.

(Part 2 — The Ghost of the Path)

Arin hit the red earth of the far ledge with a bone-jarring impact. His fingers clawed into the damp soil, roots tearing under his fingernails as momentum tried to roll him back toward the lip of the canyon.

Behind him, the sound was tectonic.

The remaining cables snapped with the report of whip-cracks, and the entire structure—decades of weathered oak and hemp—simply surrendered. It didn't just fall; it folded into the mist. Arin watched, chest heaving, as the last planks spun into the white fury below, swallowed instantly by the river's mindless hunger.

Then came the silence.

It wasn't the empty silence of the desert. It was a sharp, pressurized quiet that hummed with the ghost of the bridge. Arin lay there for a long time, his cheek pressed against the cold, iron-scented dirt, listening to the roar of the water three hundred feet below.

He was alive. But he was stranded.

The Erasure of the "Back"

He pushed himself up slowly, his muscles trembling with a post-adrenaline chill. He turned to look across the chasm.

The far side—the side he had just come from—looked like a different world. The jungle there was a wall of impenetrable green, indifferent to the fact that it had just been disconnected from him forever. There was no bridge. There was no crossing. There was only the space where a path had once existed.

In Ellmere, there was always a way back. You could turn around at the well. You could walk back down the hill. Even on the Ironcrests, the trail existed behind you, a thread of hope.

But here, the thread had been cut by the gravity of his own choices.

The realization didn't come as a panic. It came as a profound, heavy clarity. The "Bridge of No Return" wasn't just a name; it was a physical law. Every step forward from this moment was fueled by the fact that there was no longer an alternative.

The Ink of the Absolute

Arin reached into his pack. His hands were still shaking—not from the exertion, but from the realization of how thin the line between "being" and "nothing" had become.

He pulled out the journal. The leather was scuffed from the fall, stained with the red clay of the far bank. He opened it to a fresh page, the paper fluttering in the updraft of the canyon.

He didn't write about the height. He didn't write about the snap of the ropes. He wrote about the power of the broken path.

Some paths only exist once, he wrote, the ink dark and certain. *They are not roads; they are invitations to transform. Once crossed, they destroy themselves so you cannot return to the person you were before the crossing.*

He paused, looking at the empty air where the ropes had hung.

That is what makes them real, he added. *A path you can always leave is just a distraction. A path that disappears behind you... that is a destiny.*

The Forward Momentum

He closed the journal with a snap that echoed against the canyon walls.

The jungle ahead of him was darker now, the shadows stretching into long, violet fingers as the sun began to dip. It looked unforgiving. It looked uncertain. But as Arin stood up and adjusted the straps of his pack, he felt a strange, terrifying lightness.

The hesitation was gone. The second-guessing, the "what-ifs," the lingering ghost of the valley—they had all fallen into the canyon with the bridge.

He wasn't a traveler anymore. He was a force.

Arin turned away from the void. He didn't look back at the far bank. He didn't wonder how he would ever get home. Home was no longer a place in the past; it was a state of being he had to build in the future.

He stepped into the shadows of the new jungle, his boots striking the earth with a finality that matched the snap of the cables.

Forward. It was the only direction left in the world.

(Part 3 — The Heart of the Mystery)

The jungle did not thin out as Arin pushed deeper; it synchronized. The chaotic tangle of vines and rot began to give way to a terrifying, geometric precision. The trunks of the trees were no longer rough bark, but smooth, obsidian-dark pillars that felt slightly warm to the touch. The leaves overhead—once a messy canopy—now overlapped like the scales of a great, green beast, pulsing with a faint, rhythmic bioluminescence that matched the thrumming in Arin's chest.

He wasn't just walking through a forest anymore. He was walking through a machine.

The Signal in the Deep

The sound of the roaring canyon faded, replaced by a crystalline silence that tasted of ozone. Then, the "Signal" started—a low, melodic chime that seemed to vibrate directly into his skull. It wasn't music; it was a coordinate.

Arin followed it. His "Awake" vision, dormant since the desert, flared back to life. The world turned into a tapestry of silver ley lines, all of them converging on a single point in the dark.

He broke through a final wall of silver-leafed ferns and stopped.

The jungle didn't end. It circled a hollow. In the center of the clearing stood a structure that looked like a fallen star. It was a spire of ivory and gold, identical in craftsmanship to the White City, but reclaimed by the wild. Vines made of braided copper wire climbed its sides, and the base was submerged in a pool of water so clear it looked like liquid diamond.

The First Citizen

Sitting at the edge of the pool, his feet submerged in the glowing water, was a man.

He didn't look like the Navigator Elias. He didn't look like the weathered Captain of the *Virella*. He looked like a man who had been carved from the same light as the spire. His skin had a faint, iridescent sheen, and his eyes—when he turned to look at Arin—were not eyes at all. They were twin spheres of shifting, violet nebulae.

"You're the one who broke the bridge," the man said. His voice didn't travel through the air; it resonated inside Arin's mind, clear and ancient.

Arin stayed at the edge of the clearing, his hand white-knuckled on the strap of his pack. "The bridge was old. It was ready to fall."

"The bridge was a filter," the man replied, standing up. He was tall—inhumanly so—and moved with a grace that made the wind seem clumsy. "Most who reach the canyon turn back. Some try to cross and fall. But very few run *as* it breaks. That requires a specific kind of madness. Or a specific kind of truth."

The Offering of the Spire

The man gestured toward the ivory spire. A seam appeared in the smooth stone, spiraling open to reveal a chamber filled with a soft, amber glow. Inside, resting on a pedestal of floating glass, was a single, silver compass—but it had no needle. It had seven points, all of them dark.

"You have crossed the mountain, the sea, the city, and the silence," the man said, stepping closer. The air around him smelled of rain and ancient books. "You have deleted your past. Now, the question is: are you brave enough to have a future?"

Arin looked from the man to the spire. He felt the weight of the journal in his bag—the record of his struggle. He realized that this was the "Heart." This wasn't just a destination; it was the engine of the world he had been seeking.

"Who are you?" Arin asked.

"I am the Echo of what you will become," the man whispered. "If you take the next step."

The Final Line of the Chapter

Arin walked toward the water. He didn't hesitate. The "Stillness" of Ellmere was a million miles away, a ghost he no longer recognized. He stepped into the pool, the liquid diamond swirling around his boots, and reached for the seven-pointed compass.

As his fingers touched the silver metal, the first point ignited with a fierce, violet light.

He pulled out his journal, his hand steady, his heart a rhythmic engine of purpose. He wrote the final words of the chapter, the ink appearing to burn onto the page:

The mystery is not a secret to be told. It is a frequency to be matched. I have stopped looking for the door. I am becoming the key.

He closed the journal. The spire began to hum, a deep, gravitational sound that shook the very roots of the jungle. The violet light from the compass reflected in Arin's eyes, changing them, etching the map of the "Giants" into his soul.

The Bridge was gone. The Forest was watching. And for the first time, Arin Vale was home.

CHAPTER 7 - THE STRANGER WITH THE COMPASS

(Part 1 — The Valley of the Watchers)

The mountains returned, but they had shed the jagged, adolescent rage of the Ironcrests.

These peaks did not erupt from the earth in a frantic grab for the sky; they endured. They rose with a tectonic authority, layered in charcoal stone and veils of moving mist, their edges smoothed by the slow, rhythmic passage of eons. Forests of ancient, blue-black pine clung to their flanks like fur, and silver glacial streams carved lines of impossible precision through the valleys below.

There was a profound strength here. It was patient. Measured. It was the strength of something that has already seen the end of the world and decided to stay.

Arin felt the shift the moment he stepped over the final ridge of the jungle. After the emerald chaos and the scream of the falling bridge, the Valley of Oakhaven felt... composed. It wasn't safe—the sheer scale of the cliffs made that a lie—but it was settled. The air was thin and sharp, carrying the scent of woodsmoke and old snow.

Smoke meant life. And in the wild, life was a miracle.

The Reveal of the Hearth

By dusk, the village emerged from the fog like a memory returning to a mind.

It didn't appear all at once; it unfolded. Wooden longhouses, built from timber so dark it looked like iron, nestled into the natural curve of the valley floor. Their roofs were sloped against winters that Arin could only imagine, their walls scarred by wind and time.

As the light failed, lanterns flickered to life. They weren't the harsh, electric glares of the White City or the frantic torches of the road. They were soft, amber pulses—inviting, rhythmic, and grounded.

Arin entered the village. No one rushed to meet him. No one recoiled in fear. The people moved with a calm, predatory awareness, acknowledging him with a nod that said: *You are here. That is enough.* It was a place between places. A pause in the music of the journey.

The Inn of the Broken Needle

He found the inn near the village well, a structure of heavy beams that groaned a welcome as he pushed through the door. Inside, the atmosphere was a physical embrace—the roar of a massive hearth, the low vibration of baritone voices, and the rhythmic *clink* of pewter on oak.

For the first time since the "Stillness" of the valley, Arin stopped moving.

It wasn't exhaustion; he had survived worse. It was permission. The valley allowed him to exist without effort for a single, precious hour. He ate bread that tasted of earth and drank ale that tasted of the mountain, letting the heat of the fire sink into his scarred hands.

Until—he saw the Stranger.

The man sat in a far corner, illuminated by a single, dying candle. He was separate from the room, wrapped in a travel-cloak of layered wool and cured leather that had seen a dozen climates. His face was a map of experience—lines etched deep by sun, salt, and shadow. His eyes weren't looking at the fire. They were locked on his palm.

In his hand sat a compass.

It was a heavy, brass instrument, the casing battered and scratched, the glass clouded by years of condensation. But as Arin drew closer, he saw the "Blockbuster" defect.

The needle did not point. It did not settle. It spun.

It moved with a restless, frantic energy—circling the dial, slowing to a jitter, then whipping around again in a blur of polished steel. It was a machine in a state of permanent indecision.

The Honest Machine

"You're staring," the old man said. His voice wasn't a rasp; it was a low-frequency rumble, steady as the mountains outside.

Arin stopped. He didn't feel the need to apologize. The "Awake" vision in his mind was focused entirely on that spinning needle. It was the only thing in the room that felt as fast as his own thoughts.

"It's broken," Arin said.

The old man smiled, a slow unfolding of skin that didn't reach his eyes—because his eyes were already full of a different kind of light.

"Is it?" the man asked. He held the compass higher. The needle went into a manic whirl, clockwise then counter, searching for a North that didn't exist in this valley.

"It doesn't point anywhere," Arin stepped into the candle-light.

The old man finally looked up. For a second, Arin felt a phantom weight on his chest. It was the sensation of being *seen*—not as a traveler, but as a sequence of choices.

"Exactly," the old man replied.

The silence that followed was intentional. It wasn't the vacuum of the desert; it was the silence of a loaded weapon.

"Where are you going?" the man asked.

Arin opened his mouth to say *The White City*. He opened it to say *Forward*. But the spinning needle caught his eye again.

"I don't know," Arin said. The honesty of the statement felt like ice water in his veins.

The old man nodded. "Good. Most people spend their lives waiting for a needle to stop. They wait for a sign, a command, a 'True North' to tell them they are allowed to move. They wait for a certainty that the universe isn't interested in providing."

He slid the compass across the scarred wood of the table. It rattled, the needle still dancing its chaotic jig.

"There is no True North in a life worth living, Arin Vale."

The Decision Point

Arin stared at the instrument. "Then how do you know where to go?"

"You don't," the man said, leaning forward until the candle-light turned his eyes to amber. "You decide. Direction isn't something you find under a glass lens. It's something you forge with your boots."

Arin thought of the Bridge. He thought of the Seven-Pointed Star. He realized that every "Map" he had followed had been an illusion. Only the "Choices" had been solid.

"Take it," the man commanded.

"It's broken," Arin repeated, though his hand was already reaching out.

"No," the man whispered, his voice vibrating with the weight of a final truth. "It's the only honest thing in this room. It tells you the truth of the world: that the way is always moving. That you are the only thing that stays still long enough to choose."

Arin's fingers closed over the cool brass. The weight was unexpected—it felt as heavy as a mountain stone. The needle spun beneath his thumb, restless, alive, and utterly uncontrolled.

When Arin looked up, the corner was empty. The old man hadn't vanished into smoke; he had simply moved with the quiet efficiency of someone who no longer needed to be noticed.

Arin sat alone, the compass humming in his grip. Later that night, by the light of a fading hearth, he opened his journal. He wrote the words that would define the rest of his life:

Certainty is the comfort of the blind. Decision is the vision of the Awake.

He closed the book. He didn't look for North. He looked at the door.

(Part 2 — Redux — The Sentinel of the Void)

The mist did not lift as Arin climbed beyond the last, clinging blue-pines of the valley; it turned to ice.

The trail died, consumed by a causeway of seamless, obsidian-black glass that seemed to generate its own gravity. The air, already thin, became so cold it cracked against the inner lining of his lungs with the taste of ozone and old iron. The silence of the peaks was no longer peaceful; it was a pressurized hold, a tectonic breath held by the universe itself.

Then, the mountain *shifted.*

Ahead, through the swirling silver-frost, a structure emerged that was less an architecture and more a weapon. It was a gate, but it was forged from the fossils of pre-historic leviathans, braced with ribs of an unknown black metal that pulsed with a low, electromagnetic vibration. It didn't look like a passage; it looked like a trap.

And standing before it was the Guardian.

The Leviathan of the Pass

He was not a man, and he was not a shadow. He was a colossal, nine-foot tall construct of polished bone and articulated iron, a synthesis of ancient technology and organic decay. He wore no armor; he *was* the armor. Four separate arms, each ending in crushing talons, rumbled with hydraulic power. His head was a smooth, faceless dome of obsidian that reflected Arin's approach in a terrifying, fish-eye distortion.

The Guardian didn't speak. He hummed. It was a sub-bass sound that resonated in Arin's teeth, a frequency of pure, indifference.

Arin stopped. He felt the broken compass in his pocket vibrate so fast it generated a blister of heat against his thigh. He adjusted his pack, his hand tightening on the strap—and on the weight of the journal within.

The Audit of the Body

The construct did not attack. It stepped forward with a grinding, rhythmic heavy impact, its presence alone enough to generate a displacement wave of cold air. A single, metallic arm unfolded, the talons stopping inches from Arin's face.

A voice, synthesized and overlapping from a dozen processors, filled the pass. *"This threshold is not a door. It is an audit. To enter the City, you must prove the mettle of the journey that brought you to the edge of it."*

The faceless obsidian dome leaned in. *"Surrender the physical proof. Let the weight of your path determine the right of your entry."*

Arin knew what the machine meant. It was the same choice Tomas had given him, but with a mechanical finality. *Give me the journal.* Give me the memory. Let the machine process the data of your life and decide if you fit the algorithm of the Awake.

"No," Arin said, his voice flat and hard against the wind. "My life is not data. It's an act."

The Clash of Will

The Guardian hummed louder, the violet light of the gate flaring behind him. Two more arms unfolded, a pair of serrated, diamond-edged glaives sparking against the black glass floor.

"The Awake do not carry the dead weight of a remembered self," the machine rumbled. *"If you will not give the record, you must defend it. The audit will be paid in motion."*

It was a test of "Choice" as "Effort." The machine attacked with a blurring, four-armed sequence of cuts and crushing lunges.

Arin didn't have a weapon. He didn't have "V Vision" in the traditional sense. But as he had learned with the fox, in the storm, and with the "Gilded Cage," he *understood the mechanism of survival.*

He didn't fight the Guardian; he fought the gravity. He didn't try to block; he anticipated the hydraulic hiss of the pistons. He moved with the desperate, improvisational fluidity he had learned on the Bridge of No Return.

The clash was a "Blockbuster" symphony of kinetic force—steel against bone, body against glass. Arin was battered, bruised, his skin seared by the cold and the electric-field of the construct. But he did not yield. He used the very weight of his past—the rage of the Ironcrests, the endurance of the Veldt—as a source of motion.

The Decision of the Key

Arin lunged inside the spin of the diamond-glaives. He slammed his body against the primary hydraulic core of the construct's chest. The impact should have shattered his bones, but for a micro-second, he synchronized his own rhythmic purpose with the machine's frequency.

He didn't use strength. He used *impact.* He applied the lesson of the Compass: *forge the direction.*

The construct rumbled, the Faceless obsidian dome cracking as its internal logic core struggled to compute an action that defied an algorithm. It stepped back.

"The audit is... complete," the machine synthesized, its voice now layered with static. *"Mettle is verified. A memory that can defend its own right to exist is not a burden. It is a key."*

The Guardian lowered its arms and stepped aside, the massive, leviathan gate spiraling open behind it. Arin staggered, his body broken but his will absolutely intact. He reached back and touched his bag, his fingers tracing the spine of the journal.

I didn't leave you behind, he thought, the first spark of the Seven-Pointed Star igniting in his eyes. *I took you with me.*

Arin stepped into the soft, silent light of the White City. Behind him, the Sentinel of the Void hummed its dynamic approval as the leviathan gate closed, sealing the past into the present. Arin Vale had reached the end. But the journal knew...

it was only Chapter 1.

CHAPTER 8 - THE FOREST OF DOUBT

(Part 1 — The Fractured Labyrinth)

The forest did not begin with trees; it began with the sudden, violent death of Perspective.

At first, it appeared as a harmless stretch of woodland, its edges soft and dappled with the amber light of late afternoon. A faint path—worn just enough to suggest the passage of ghosts—led inward. It didn't resist Arin; it didn't growl like the jungle or press like the desert. It invited him in with the terrifying courtesy of a trap that has already been sprung.

Arin stepped inside, and the universe suffered a stroke.

The air didn't just cool; it thickened into a pressurized gel that tasted of copper and ancient, exhaled breath. The outside world was severed—not by distance, but by a sudden, absolute acoustic wall. No wind. No birds. No rustle of his own pack. Just a high-pitched, electric hum that seemed to originate from the marrow of his own bones.

The Geometry of the Loop

The path, once a clear promise of direction, began to behave unnaturally.

Arin walked for what felt like an hour, his eyes fixed on a specific, lightning-scarred oak ahead. He blinked, and the oak was behind him. He turned, and it was to his left. He checked the sun, but the light was no longer coming from the sky; it was bleeding out of the leaves themselves, a sour, subterranean green that cast no shadows.

He stopped. He turned to look back at the entrance.

Gone. Not distant. Not obscured. The forest had simply closed its teeth behind him. Every direction was now an identical corridor of grey-barked trees whose trunks twisted into patterns that looked like screaming faces caught in mid-sentence.

He pulled the brass compass from his pocket. The needle wasn't just spinning now; it was vibrating so violently it struck the glass casing with a frantic *tic-tic-tic-tic*—the sound of a heart having a panic attack.

The Siege of the Internal Voice

"Is this the right way?"

The thought didn't feel like his own. It felt projected into his skull by the trees.

"Should you turn back? What if the Guardian was wrong? What if the White City is just another version of the City of Easy Choices?"

Arin slowed, his boots sinking into a moss that felt like wet velvet. The silence pressed in, amplifying the doubt until it was louder than the storm on the *Virella*. In the desert, the silence had been a mirror; here, it was an inquisitor. It didn't just show him his regrets—it weaponized them.

"You're walking in circles," the voice whispered, sounding like a thousand dry leaves skittering across stone. "You've been here before. This tree. This root. This failure."

He stopped. He sat down on a fallen log, and for a moment, the "Stillness" of Ellmere returned to claim him. It felt reasonable to wait. It felt logical to stay still until a sign appeared—a bird, a light, a change in the wind.

But as the moss began to creep over his boots, as the "Ease" of surrender began to numb his legs, he realized the "Blockbuster" horror of the forest.

The forest didn't trap people with thorns. It trapped them with **Hesitation**.

Every skeleton he might find in these woods wouldn't be a victim of a predator; it would be the remains of someone who had decided to wait for a certainty that never arrived.

The Kinetic Break-Out

Arin stood up. The movement felt like breaking through a layer of ice.

He looked at the compass—the needle still a blur of indecision—and he smiled. It was a jagged, dangerous expression. He didn't need the needle to stop. He needed it to stay broken.

"Direction," Arin whispered to the screaming trees, "is a choice, not a discovery."

He didn't pick a path. He *made* one.

He turned toward the thickest tangle of grey bark and began to walk. He didn't scan the horizon for landmarks. He didn't look back to see if he was moving in a straight line. He focused entirely on the kinetic rhythm of the *Step*.

Step. Step. Step.

The doubt roared. The trees seemed to lean in, their branches clawing at his pack, the forest floor shifting to trip his stride. The "Sensory Distortion" reached its peak—the world around him began to blur into a smear of grey and green, time stretching and snapping like a frayed rope.

"You're wrong!" the forest shrieked through the wind. "You're lost! You're wasting the only life you have!"

Arin didn't listen. He synchronized his breathing with the vibration of the compass. He stopped being a man looking for a way out and became a bullet moving through a target.

And then—the resistance snapped.

The air thinned. The sour green light was lanced by a beam of pure, white-gold sun. The pressure in his ears popped, and the high-pitched hum was replaced by the glorious, chaotic noise of the world: a hawk screaming, wind rushing through grass, and the sound of his own heavy, triumphant breathing.

He stepped out of the tree-line.

Behind him, the Forest of Doubt looked small—a mere patch of woodland between two ridges. It wasn't a labyrinth; it was a threshold.

Arin pulled out his journal. His hand didn't tremble. He wrote with the force of a man carving his name into history:

Doubt is not a sign to stop. It is the friction required to prove you are moving. The way out was never hidden; it was forged.

He closed the book. Ahead of him, the White City finally sat on the horizon, no longer a dream or a mystery, but a destination.

Arin Vale took a step forward. He didn't look back. He didn't need to. He was finally, absolutely, Awake.

(Part 2 — The Resonant Threshold)

The open land beyond the tree-line was not the meadow Arin had expected. It was a shelf of grey, weathered granite that sloped sharply downward, tucked between two gargantuan ridges that seemed to be trying to crush the very air between them. The White City still sat on the horizon, but it was framed now by a new distortion. The air above the valley didn't just shimmer; it vibrated. A low-frequency hum, deeper than the one in the forest, began to rattle the brass casing of the compass in Arin's pocket.

He didn't just hear the sound. He felt it in his marrow. It was the sound of the earth breathing through a straw.

The Mouth of the Abyss

As he descended the granite slope, the wind began to howl, but not with the chaos of the sea. This was a channeled, surgical wind, pulled into a massive obsidian archway at the base of the eastern ridge.

The archway was natural, yet its symmetry was terrifying. It looked like a throat.

Arin stopped at the lip of the descent. The "Awake" vision flared, turning the shadows of the archway into a swirling vortex of silver and violet energy. This wasn't just a cave; it was a conduit. The Ley Lines he had followed through the jungle didn't just end at the City; they flowed *through* this mountain.

He pulled out the journal. The ink on the previous page was still damp, but the air here was so dry it felt like it was trying to suck the very words off the paper.

Movement solved the forest, he wrote, his hand vibrating with the frequency of the stone. *But movement alone is a blind force. To reach the City, I must not only move; I must listen.*

The Symphony of the Shadow

He stepped into the shadows of the arch.

The transition was instantaneous. The gold-white sun of the valley was extinguished, replaced by a soft, ambient phosphorescence that clung to the damp walls. But it was the sound that defined the space.

Every step Arin took didn't just echo; it multiplied.

The sound of his boot hitting the stone traveled down the tunnel, hit a bend, and returned as a distorted, metallic chime. His breath sounded like a bellows. The rustle of his pack sounded like a landslide. The cave wasn't just reflecting sound; it was amplifying the "Frequency" of his presence.

He looked ahead. The tunnel didn't go straight. It spiraled downward in a perfect, logarithmic curve.

The Convergence of Voices

Deep within the dark, a new sound began to emerge. It wasn't the wind, and it wasn't his own movement.

It was a chorus.

Thousands of overlapping whispers, layered like the scales of a serpent, drifted up from the depths. They weren't words—not yet. They were the tonal ghosts of everyone who had ever stood at this threshold. He heard the "Stillness" of Ellmere. He heard the "Roar" of the *Virella*. He heard the "Laughter" of Aurelia.

The Cave of Echoes was not a place of silence. It was a place where the past was recycled into a physical force.

Arin gripped the strap of his pack, feeling the weight of the journal against his spine. He realized that the Forest of Doubt had been the test of his "Will." This cave would be the test of his "Truth."

He stepped deeper into the spiral, the light of the entrance shrinking into a tiny, white needle-point behind him. The violet glow of the compass intensified, illuminating the path ahead—a path paved with the crystalline resonance of a thousand stories.

He didn't look back. He didn't hesitate. He walked into the roar of the echoes, ready to hear the one voice he had been avoiding for a lifetime.

His own.

CHAPTER 9 - THE CAVE OF ECHOES

(Part 1 — The Acoustic Archaeology)

The land did not merely change; it collapsed into a singular, predatory focus. The sky dimmed without the mercy of clouds, turning a bruised, atmospheric purple. The wind didn't just quiet—it died, as if the world had collectively held its breath. Beneath Arin's boots, the earth transitioned from resilient granite to a dead, obsidian-slick stone that felt as cold as a deep-sea trench.

The horizon tightened. The vastness he had conquered after the forest began to fold inward, the mountains leaning in like colossal judges. The path led him into a throat of rising stone—a valley that didn't just guide passage, it demanded it.

Then, he saw the Entrance.

It was a jagged, vertical wound in the cliff face, its edges torn and raw. The darkness within wasn't the absence of light; it was a physical substance—a dense, light-eating fog that refused to reflect the world outside.

Arin stopped. The silence here was a "Blockbuster" vacuum. No wind, no insects, no heartbeat. Just a pressurized stillness that felt like it was listening to the very electricity in his nerves.

The Descent into the Mouth

The temperature plummeted forty degrees the moment Arin crossed the threshold. A cold, damp exhalation puffed out from the depths, smelling of ancient rain and copper.

He didn't hesitate out of fear. He hesitated out of **Recognition**. Every step of the mountain, every wave of the sea, every shadow of the city had been a preamble to this specific darkness. He stepped inside.

The world behind him was deleted. The entrance didn't just fade; it vanished as if the mountain had swallowed the light. Arin moved forward, his fingers brushing the weeping stone walls. They felt rhythmic, vibrating with a low-frequency thrum that made the brass compass in his pocket rattle like a trapped bird.

Step. Step. Step.

The echo didn't just return. It **Evolved**.

The sound of his boot hitting the stone lingered three seconds too long. It warped. The *click* of the heel became a *snap*. The *shuffle* of the sole became a *hiss*. The cave was not just repeating him; it was remixing him.

The Auditory Siege

"Hello?" Arin whispered.

The word left his lips and became a weapon. It spun away into the darkness, bouncing off the invisible geometry of the vault, returning in a thousand different voices.

"Hello... hello... hello..."

But the fourth echo wasn't his voice. It was Tomas's. The fifth was his father's. The sixth was the melodic, deceptive lilt of the woman from the City of Easy Choices.

"Who's there?" he shouted, his voice cracking the pressurized air.

The cave didn't just answer; it **Excavated**.

"You never cared," a voice hissed from the ceiling. It was Arin's own voice, but from five years ago—the day he had turned his back on the valley's needs to focus on his own safety.

Arin froze. The "Awake" vision flared, but it didn't show him the path. it showed him the **Vibrations of his own Regrets**. The air was thick with glowing, silver threads of sound—visible memories hanging in the dark like spiderwebs.

"You said you'd stay," a softer voice wept from the floor. *"You forgot."*

"No," Arin gritted out, his hands slamming against his ears.

But the cave was a "Blockbuster" amplifier. It bypassed his hands and spoke directly to his skull. It wasn't an argument; it was a **Data-Dump of the Soul**. Every promise unkept, every word spoken in anger, every moment he had chosen "Stillness" over "Truth" erupted from the stone.

"You didn't listen." "You could have stayed." "You walked away."

The voices circled him in a tectonic whirlwind, the frequency rising until the stone itself seemed to scream.

The Physics of Honesty

Arin dropped to his knees. The weight of the sound was physical—it felt like tons of rock pressing against his chest. He had faced the storm on the *Virella*, but that was just water. This was the **Gravity of a Lived Life**.

"ENOUGH!" he roared.

The word exploded. It hit the walls with the force of a percussion grenade. The echoes shattered. The whispers died. For a heartbeat, there was a vacuum of absolute, terrifying silence.

And then, one final voice spoke. It didn't shout. It didn't whisper. It was steady, resonant, and impossibly clear. It came from the compass in his pocket.

"You knew."

The words didn't accuse. They **Revealed**.

Arin lowered his hands. He realized the cave wasn't a monster; it was a **Reflector**. It was a high-altitude hall of mirrors for the ears. It wasn't inventing his sins; it was just playing back the record he had been trying to erase since Ellmere.

He stopped fighting the sound. He stood up, his body bruised by the frequency but his mind suddenly, violently clear. He didn't deny the voices. He **Claimed** them.

"Yes," he whispered to the dark. "I knew. I forgot. I walked away. And I am still here."

The silver threads of sound didn't vanish—they **Integrated**. They flowed toward him, spiraling into the "Awake" light behind his eyes. The past wasn't a weight to be dropped; it was the fuel for the engine.

Ahead, a faint, crystalline light appeared. Not the sun. Something older. The light of the White City, seen through the exit of the soul.

Arin walked toward it. Each step no longer echoed with doubt. It echoed with **Purpose**.

(Part 2 — The Threshold of Reaping)

The crystalline light at the end of the tunnel didn't grow warmer as Arin approached; it grew sharper. It was a cold, surgical blue that seemed to cut through the lingering echoes of his past, peeling away the last of the cave's humid introspection.
As he took the final step out of the obsidian throat, the sound of his own heart—which had been a rhythmic drum in the dark—suddenly felt too loud for the world he had entered.

He stepped out onto a ledge of white quartz, suspended five thousand feet above a basin that should not have existed.

The Geography of the End

Below him lay The Valley of Consequences.

It was a perfect, geometric crater, miles wide, carved into the very roots of the world. But it wasn't filled with the lush forests of the Oakhaven or the shimmering towers of the White City he had dreamed of. It was a graveyard of abandoned momentum.

The "Awake" vision flared in Arin's eyes, but it didn't show him the silver ley lines of power. It showed him **Static**. The air in the valley was thick with frozen sound—shards of light that looked like shattered glass, hanging motionless in the atmosphere.

"It's beautiful, isn't it?"

The voice didn't come from the cave. It came from the ledge beside him.

Arin spun, his hand instinctively reaching for the heavy brass compass in his pocket. Standing at the very edge of the quartz precipice was a figure clad in robes of woven smoke. They didn't have a face—only a mask of polished silver that reflected the dead, blue sky.

The Audit of the World

"The Cave showed you your own voice," the Figure said, its tone as flat and lethal as a razor. "But the Valley... the Valley shows you the weight of your footprints."

The Figure gestured toward the crater below. Arin looked down, and his stomach turned.

He saw them now. Tiny, flickering lights moving through the frozen shards of the valley floor. They weren't people. They were **Echoes of Decisions**. He saw the ghost of the *Virella* breaking against a spectral reef. He saw a version of himself still sitting in the *Café of the Sun*, slowly turning to marble. He saw the bridge he had broken, still falling, forever suspended in the moment of its collapse.

"Every choice you made to get here didn't just change you, Arin Vale," the Figure whispered, stepping closer. The air around them smelled of ozone and scorched paper. "It changed the world. You broke the bridge to save yourself. You left the village to find your truth. You walked through the forest and left the doubt behind."

The Figure's silver mask tilted.

"But where do you think the doubt went? Where do you think the bridge fell? Everything you discarded to become 'Awake' has been gathered here. In the Valley of Consequences, nothing is ever truly lost. It is simply... stored."

The Warning of the White City

Above the crater, the White City finally appeared, floating on a cushion of violet energy. It was magnificent—a masterpiece of light and logic. But from this height, Arin could see the truth.

The City wasn't powered by the stars. It was powered by the **Debt** of the valley below. The violet ley lines were anchored into the shards of discarded lives and broken promises.

"To enter the City is to claim the throne of what you've destroyed," the Figure said, their hand extending toward the descent. "You have integrated your past, yes. But are you ready to face the cost of your future?"

The ground beneath the quartz ledge groaned. A massive, tectonic shift echoed from the bottom of the crater. The frozen shards began to vibrate. The "Static" was waking up.

Arin looked at his journal, then at the floating spires of his obsession. The suspense wasn't in the danger of the height; it was in the realization that the journey wasn't over. It was just getting heavy.

The first shard of frozen sound—a jagged, glowing scream from his time in the desert—broke free and began to rise toward the ledge.

The audit had begun.

CHAPTER 10 - THE VALLEY OF CONSEQUENCES

(The Harvest of Choice)

The valley did not announce itself. It revealed itself slowly—like a long-suppressed truth finally finding its voice.

After the claustrophobic resonance of the Cave, the world felt agonizingly sharp. The air was no longer thick with the static of the dead; it was charged with the electricity of the living. Arin walked for days through terrain that no longer fought him, but no longer coddled him either. The ground was honest—hard stone transitioning into resilient, deep-emerald grass.

He carried less now. The internal ghosts of the Cave hadn't followed him into the light, but their weight had been replaced by a dense, golden clarity.

Then, the horizon broke open.

Arin stopped at the crest of the final ridge. Below him, the valley stretched for miles, a vast basin carved into the cradle of the world. It wasn't the sterile, floating White City of his hallucinations. It was something infinitely more powerful.

It was a **Settlement in Motion**.

The Kinetic Civilization

The valley was alive with a rhythmic, industrial beauty. Huge, reinforced transport vessels—hybrids of the *Virella's* naval grit and the White City's elegant geometry—moved across the plains. These were not permanent structures; they were a caravan of civilizations, an organized exodus of people who had turned "Survival" into "Progress."

Smoke curled from mobile forges. Huge windmills, built from salvaged ship-masts and desert silk, turned in the breeze. Thousands of voices carried across the open space—not as a chaotic roar, but as a focused, symphonic hum.

Arin stepped down the slope, his heart hammering against his ribs. He saw people moving with an intentionality he had never witnessed in the "Stillness" of his home or the "Detachment" of Aurelia. These were people who had built a world with their bare hands.

"Arin?"

The voice cut through the ambient noise of the forges like a bell. Clear. Grounded. Impossible.

Arin turned, and his breath left him in a ragged gasp.

The Return of the Anchor

Standing before him was a man who looked like he had been forged from the very mountains they had once tried to escape.

It was **Tomas**.

But the broken, desperate man Arin had dragged through the snow was gone. This Tomas stood with the quiet authority of an oak. His shoulders were broad, his eyes clear of the fog of pain. He wore a captain's longcoat of rugged leather, and he stood without a crutch.

Arin's gaze dropped to Tomas's leg. It was encased in a brilliant, articulated brace of silver and steel—a masterpiece of engineering that moved with a faint, hydraulic hiss.

"You made it," Tomas said. A slow, weathered smile broke across his face—a smile that held the weight of years.

"You're walking," Arin whispered, the words feeling small in the face of such a miracle.

Tomas laughed, a deep, resonant sound. "Eventually. It took time. It took the kind of help you only find when you're forced to start over. It took a second chance I didn't think I deserved."

He gestured to the sprawling, kinetic city around them. "This? This is what happens when someone decides not to leave the world behind. You saved me, Arin. And in doing so, you saved everyone I've helped since."

The Captain of the Storm

They walked through the heart of the caravan. People acknowledged Tomas with a respect that wasn't demanded, but earned—a quiet nod of the head from a blacksmith, a wave from a navigator.

At the far end of the valley, standing atop the bridge of a massive, land-crawling vessel, was a figure that made Arin's pulse spike.

It was the **Deckhand**. The boy from the *Virella* who had frozen in the face of the kraken and the gale.

He was a boy no longer. He was a Captain.

He stood tall, his hands scarred and steady on a massive brass railing. When he saw Arin, the recognition was an electric shock. He descended the ladder in a blur of practiced motion, stopping inches from Arin.

“You were on the *Virella*,” the Captain said, his voice now a steady baritone. “The man who wouldn't let go of the rope.”

“And you’re the one who pulled,” Arin replied.

The Captain looked out over his crew, his eyes reflecting the three suns of the valley. “I thought I’d freeze forever that night. I thought fear was a cage. But you made me move. And because the ship didn't sink, we found this place. Because you held on, we learned how to build.”

The Final Entry

Arin felt the "Blockbuster" scale of the realization hit him like a physical blow. A single decision on a snowy mountain. A single choice to hold a rope in a storm. These weren't isolated events. They were the **First Ripples**.

He pulled out his journal. The leather was ruined, the pages stained with salt, sand, and blood. But as he opened it, the words felt like they were glowing.

He wrote the final lines with a hand that had stopped trembling:

A single decision does not end in the moment it is made. It travels. It echoes through people, through time, and through lives we may never see. Responsibility is not a weight to be carried—it is the compass by which we build the future.

He closed the journal.

The White City still sat on the horizon, but Arin didn't look at it. He didn't need the "Awake" vision anymore. He was the vision.

He took a step forward into the heart of the valley. He wasn't a traveler anymore. He was a Founder. And for the first time in his life, Arin Vale knew exactly where he was going.

CHAPTER 11 - THE LAST UNWRITTEN PAGE

(The Event Horizon)

The world did not end with a line. It ended with a Vast, Golden Silence.

Arin felt the atmospheric shift long before the horizon gave up its secrets. It was a thinning of the fundamental laws of reality—the air lost its humidity, the sound lost its echo, and the very gravity beneath his boots seemed to loosen its grip, as if the earth itself was hesitant to claim the space ahead.

For days, the terrain of the Valley of Consequences had smoothed into a high, scorched-white plateau. The trees had retreated, the streams had vanished into the stone, and the wind had been stripped of its scent, leaving only the raw, electric taste of the void.

Then, he reached it. The Terminus.

The Edge of the Infinite

The cliff did not merely rise; it Severed.

It was a vertical wall of obsidian and starlight-colored stone that dropped five miles into a sea that defied every map Arin had ever seen. This was not the gray, churning water of the *Virella's* voyage. This was the Abyssal Constant—a sapphire-dark expanse so vast it didn't meet the sky; it consumed it. The horizon was not a line, but a gradient where liquid became light.

Arin stepped to the very lip of the precipice.

The wind met him with a deep, subsonic thrum—a vibration that felt like the breathing of the universe. It didn't push him; it anchored him. Below, the waves shattered against the base of the cliff with a sound like collapsing stars—relentless, rhythmic, and terrifyingly patient.

This was Time made visible. This was the end of the "Path."

The Audit of the Leather

Arin slowly removed the journal from his bag.

The book was no longer just paper and hide. It was a Vessel. It felt heavy with the kinetic energy of the mountain, the salt of the sea, and the psychic resonance of the Cave. The leather was scarred, stained, and beautiful—a physical shadow of the man holding it.

He opened it.

The pages whipped in the high-altitude gale, a frantic blur of his own evolution.

- *Today I begin.* (The boy in the snow.)
- *The Ironcrests.* (The break of the bone.)
- *The Storm.* (The grip of the rope.)
- *The Desert.* (The death of the ego.)
- *The Bridge.* (The burning of the return.)

He turned the pages faster and faster until he hit the wall.

The Final Page.

It was a stark, terrifying white. Against the backdrop of the sapphire sea and the obsidian cliff, that blank space felt like a scream. It didn't feel empty; it felt Urgent. It was the only space in the world that hadn't been conquered by his decisions.

The Physics of the Final Word

Arin held the pen, his hand suspended over the paper. The "Awake" vision flared one last time —not to show him a destination, but to show him the Fragility of the Present.

He realized the "Blockbuster" deception of his journey: He had spent months writing *after* the fact—recording the past to justify the future. But standing at the edge of the world, he understood that the final page doesn't wait for your permission to arrive. It isn't a chapter break; it's a Closing Shutter.

Life doesn't offer a "The End" banner. It offers a Moment, and then it offers Nothing.

The realization hit him with a cinematic clarity. If the last page could be claimed by the wind at any second, then the words currently being written were the only ones that actually existed.

The Final Inscription

He lowered the pen. He didn't rush. He didn't look for a grand philosophy to summarize his life. He looked at the sea, let the spray of the infinite mist hit his face, and wrote with the calm precision of a man who had finally stopped running.

"The last page is never marked."

He watched the ink soak into the fibers, turning from a wet sheen to a permanent part of the world's record.

"And that is why every moment must be lived as if it is the one that remains. Not as a conclusion, but as the entirety."

He closed the journal. The sound of the cover meeting the pages was a dull, final thud that cut through the roar of the sea.

The Leap into the Light

Arin didn't put the journal back in his bag. He held it against his chest. He stepped another inch closer to the drop, his toes hanging over the five-mile void.

He wasn't looking for what came next. He wasn't searching for the White City or a way home. He was simply Present. He was the mountain, the wind, and the ink. He was a man who had stopped being a "Traveler" and had become the Journey itself.

The final page was no longer blank. It was full of the only thing that mattered: The Decision to be Here.

Arin Vale looked out at the blurred horizon where the sea became the sky, smiled at the beautiful, terrifying uncertainty of it all, and took a breath.

The story was over. The life was just beginning.

CHAPTER 12 - THE READER OF HIS OWN LIFE

(The Quiet Resolution)

Ellmere had not changed.

That was the first "Blockbuster" realization—a terrifying, static perfection. The road into the valley curved with the exact, mindless geometry Arin had memorized as a boy. The hill stood in the distance, a silent sentinel that had never moved, never bled, and never doubted.

The air was the same: a thick, sweet stagnation that tasted of unbaked bread and forgotten dreams. It was the "Stillness" he had once fled, and as he stood at the town's edge, it felt like a physical weight pressing against his scarred chest.

He looked down at his boots—caked with the red clay of the Bridge, the white salt of the sea, and the obsidian dust of the Cave. He was a walking map of the world's violence and beauty.

And Ellmere didn't even notice.

The Invisibility of the Transformed

Arin stepped forward. Each footfall was a tectonic event in his own mind, but to the town, he was a ghost.

The baker stood behind his counter, his hands moving in the same rhythmic, circular motion he had used for forty years. Children—new faces, yet identical in their frantic, directionless joy—ran the same paths. The clocktower chimed, a steady, mechanical heartbeat that suggested nothing of importance had happened since the dawn of time.

It was humbling. The world had not paused for his enlightenment. The "Valley of Consequences" he had helped build was a thousand miles away, and here, the ripple had not yet arrived.

He reached the corner where the wooden shop stood. The sign for the bookseller still hung slightly crooked, a frozen defect in a world that refused to evolve.

The Final Mirror

"Arin?"

The voice was an anchor. It was older, frayed at the edges like a well-loved map, but its frequency matched the vibration in his bones.

He turned. **Mira** stood in the doorway.

She hadn't crossed the sea, but she had lived. The lines at the corners of her eyes were the records of a thousand sunsets; the silver in her hair was the dust of a thousand quiet days. Her eyes, however, were the same—deep, observant, and devoid of the "Stillness" that plagued the rest of the town.

She didn't gasp. She didn't drop her broom. She looked at him with the terrifying clarity of someone who had been reading him even in his absence.

“You look...” she started, her voice catching on the scale of the man before her.

“Different?” Arin offered. His voice was a baritone rumble now, shaped by the wind of the high peaks.

Mira shook her head slowly, a single, sharp tear tracking through the silver light. “No. Finished.”

The Transaction of Truth

They sat on the old wooden bench. The wood felt small beneath him—the world itself felt like a garment he had outgrown. Neither spoke for a long time. The town's rhythm continued around them, a shallow melody compared to the symphony Arin carried in his skull.

“Was it worth it?” Mira asked.

It was the only question that mattered. Arin didn't answer with words. He reached into his bag and pulled out the **Journal**.

It was a "Blockbuster" artifact now. The leather was scuffed to a dark, oily sheen; the edges of the pages were swollen with humidity and heat. It looked like it had been pulled from a shipwreck, which, in a way, it had.

He handed it to her.

Mira took it with a reverence usually reserved for religious icons. She opened it, and the smell of the world—ozone, pine, salt, and sun—erupted into the stale air of Ellmere. She didn't just read the words; she felt the weight of the ink. She saw the "Seven-Pointed Star." She saw the names of the "Awake."

She reached the final page.

"The last page is never marked."

She closed the book, her fingers lingering on the cover as if trying to pulse-check the life within it.

The Reader and the Writer

“Life,” Arin said, his gaze fixed on the horizon that had once been his prison, “is not about writing perfect pages. It’s about writing them **consciously**.”

The wind moved then—not the frantic gale of the storm, but a deliberate, cool breath from the mountains. It caught the journal in Mira’s lap, flipping the pages until it hit the very end.

There was no more white paper. No more "what-ifs."

Arin sat there, and for the first time, the "Stillness" of Ellmere didn't feel like a threat. It felt like a frame. He was no longer a character waiting for his story to begin; he was the author who had finished the first volume.

He wasn't running from the horizon anymore. He *was* the horizon.

He closed his eyes, and in the darkness, he could still hear the waves of the infinite sea crashing against the obsidian cliff. He could still feel the warmth of the White City. He had brought them all back with him.

Arin Vale opened his eyes. He didn't need to begin again. He had already written a life.

THE END

ABOUT THE AUTHOR

Nitin Narendra Jawale (Krg)

Nitin Jawale writes from the edge of awareness—the place where thoughts turn inward and refuse to stay quiet.

His words are not meant to guide, but to confront. They move through silence, hesitation, and the irreversible nature of choice. There are no heroes here, no clean endings—only reflections that stay longer than expected.

In Ink of the Irreversible, the lines are not written to be remembered. They are written because they cannot be undone.

www.ingramcontent.com/pod-product-compliance
Ingram Content Group UK Ltd.
Pitfield, Milton Keynes, MK11 3LW, UK
UKHW061547190726
13845UKWH00030B/1067

9 789357 827133